OXFORD STUDENT TEXTS
Series Editor: Victor Lee

✳

Geoffrey Chaucer
General Prologue to The Canterbury Tales

✳

Edited by
Dr Peter Mack and Chris Walton

D0828898

Oxford University Press
1994

Oxford University Press, Walton Street, Oxford OX2 6DP

Oxford New York Toronto
Delhi Bombay Calcutta Madras Karachi
Kuala Lumpur Singapore Hong Kong Tokyo
Nairobi Dar es Salaam Cape Town
Melbourne Auckland Madrid

and associated companies in
Berlin Ibadan

Oxford is a trade mark of Oxford University Press

First published by Oxford University Press
ISBN 0 19 831967 3

Typeset by Pentacor PLC
Printed and bound in Great Britain by
Butler & Tanner Ltd, Frome and London

The publishers would like to thank the following for permission to
reproduce photographs:

Canterbury Cathedral/Bridgeman Art Library Ltd p.130 top;
Courtauld Institute of Art p.130 bottom; Huntington Library, San
Marino, California p.129; The Mansell Collection pp.127, 128
both.

The cover illustration is by Susan Scott.

Contents

Acknowledgements

Peter Mack would like to acknowledge the help he received in compiling the notes from the critical works and editions listed in Further Reading, and from his colleagues, Gloria Cigman and Bill Whitehead. He is grateful to Robert Burchfield for his comments on the Note on Chaucer's English. Chris Walton would like to thank Claire Fidler and his A-level students for their comments on the Approaches, Erica Holley for valuable historical resources, and Barbara Mitchell for providing critical material. Both editors would like to thank Victor Lee and Lucy Hooper, for their constructive criticism and advice. The text is taken from L. D. Benson ed., *The Riverside Chaucer* (Cambridge, Mass, 1987), with permission.

Editors

Dr Victor Lee the series editor, read English at University College, Cardiff. He was later awarded his doctorate at the University of Oxford. He has taught at secondary and tertiary level, and is currently working at the Open University. Victor Lee's experience as an examiner is very wide: he has been a Chief Examiner in English A-level for three different boards stretching over a period of twenty years.

Dr Peter Mack read English at St Peter's College, Oxford and went on to gain an MPhil and PhD in Renaissance Studies from The Warburg Institute, University of London. He has examined English at O and A-level as well as for the International Baccalaureate. Since 1979 he has taught the First Year Medieval English Literature Course in the Department of English at Warwick University.

Chris Walton Chris Walton read English Literature and Philosophy at Leeds University. Currently, he teaches English at a comprehensive school in Wiltshire, where he has been responsible for the development of a modular A-level English syllabus. He recently gained an MPhil in classroom research at Bath University.

Foreword

Oxford Student Texts are specifically aimed at presenting poetry and drama to an audience which is studying English Literature at an advanced level. Each text is designed as an integrated whole consisting of three main parts. The poetry or the play is always placed first to stress its importance and to encourage students to enjoy it without secondary critical material of any kind. When help is needed on other occasions, the second and third parts of these texts, the Notes and the Approaches provide it.

The Notes perform two functions. First, they provide information and explain allusions. Secondly, and this is where they differ from most texts at this level, they often raise questions of central concern to the interpretation of the poem or the play being dealt with, particularly in the use of a general note placed at the beginning of the particular notes.

The third part, the Approaches section, deals with major issues of response to the particular selection of poetry or drama, as opposed to the work of the writer as a whole. One of the major aims of this part of the text is to emphasize that there is no one right answer to interpretation, but a series of approaches. Readers are given guidance as to what counts as evidence, but, in the end, left to make up their mind as to which are the most suitable interpretations, or to add their own.

To help achieve this, the Approaches section contains a number of activity-discussion sequences, although it must be stressed that these are optional. Significant issues about the poetry or the play are raised in these activities. Readers are invited to tackle these activities before proceeding to the discussion section where possible responses to the questions raised in the activities are considered. Their main function is to engage readers actively in the ideas of the text. However, these activity-discussion sequences are so arranged that, if readers wish to treat the Approaches as continuous prose and not attempt the activities, they can.

At the end of each text there is also a list of Tasks. Whereas the activity-discussion sequences are aimed at increasing understanding of the literary work itself, these tasks are intended to help explore ideas about the poetry or the play after the student has completed the reading of the work and the studying of the Notes and Approaches. These tasks are particularly helpful for coursework projects or in preparing for an examination.

Victor Lee   *Series Editor*

General Prologue to
The Canterbury Tales

Here bygynneth the Book of the Tales of Caunterbury.

Whan that Aprill with his shoures soote
The droghte of March hath perced to the roote,
And bathed every veyne in swich licour
Of which vertu engendred is the flour;
5 Whan Zephirus eek with his sweete breeth
Inspired hath in every holt and heeth
The tendre croppes, and the yonge sonne
Hath in the Ram his half cours yronne,
And smale foweles maken melodye,
10 That slepen al the nyght with open ye
(So priketh hem nature in hir corages),
Thanne longen folk to goon on pilgrimages,
And palmeres for to seken straunge strondes,
To ferne halwes, kowthe in sondry londes;
15 And specially from every shires ende
Of Engelond to Caunterbury they wende,
The hooly blisful martir for to seke,
That hem hath holpen whan that they were seeke.
    Bifil that in that seson on a day,
20 In Southwerk at the Tabard as I lay
Redy to wenden on my pilgrymage
To Caunterbury with ful devout corage,
At nyght was come into that hostelrye
Wel nyne and twenty in a compaignye
25 Of sondry folk, by aventure yfalle
In felaweshipe, and pilgrimes were they alle,
That toward Caunterbury wolden ryde.
The chambres and the stables weren wyde,

And wel we weren esed atte beste.
30   And shortly, whan the sonne was to reste,
So hadde I spoken with hem everichon
That I was of hir felaweshipe anon,
And made forward erly for to ryse,
To take oure wey ther as I yow devyse.
35   But nathelees, whil I have tyme and space,
Er that I ferther in this tale pace,
Me thynketh it acordaunt to resoun
To telle yow al the condicioun
Of ech of hem, so as it semed me,
40   And whiche they weren, and of what degree,
And eek in what array that they were inne;
And at a knyght than wol I first bigynne.
A KNYGHT ther was, and that a worthy man,
That fro the tyme that he first bigan
45   To riden out, he loved chivalrie,
Trouthe and honour, fredom and curteisie.
Ful worthy was he in his lordes werre,
And therto hadde he riden, no man ferre,
As wel in cristendom as in hethenesse,
50   And evere honoured for his worthynesse;
At Alisaundre he was whan it was wonne.
Ful ofte tyme he hadde the bord bigonne
Aboven alle nacions in Pruce;
In Lettow hadde he reysed and in Ruce,
55   No Cristen man so ofte of his degree.
In Gernade at the seege eek hadde he be
Of Algezir, and riden in Belmarye.
At Lyeys was he and at Satalye,
Whan they were wonne, and in the Grete See
60   At many a noble armee hadde he be.
At mortal batailles hadde he been fiftene,
And foughten for oure feith at Tramyssene

In lystes thries, and ay slayn his foo.
This ilke worthy knyght hadde been also
65 Somtyme with the lord of Palatye
Agayn another hethen in Turkye;
And everemoore he hadde a sovereyn prys.
And though that he were worthy, he was wys,
And of his port as meeke as is a mayde.
70 He nevere yet no vileynye ne sayde
In al his lyf unto no maner wight.
He was a verray, parfit gentil knyght.
But for to tellen yow of his array,
His hors were goode, but he was nat gay.
75 Of fustian he wered a gypon
Al bismotered with his habergeon,
For he was late ycome from his viage,
And wente for to doon his pilgrymage.
      With hym ther was his sone, a yong SQUIER,
80 A lovyere and a lusty bacheler,
With lokkes crulle as they were leyd in presse.
Of twenty yeer of age he was, I gesse.
Of his stature he was of evene lengthe,
And wonderly delyvere, and of greet strengthe.
85 And he hadde been somtyme in chyvachie
In Flaundres, in Artoys, and Pycardie,
And born hym weel, as of so litel space,
In hope to stonden in his lady grace.
Embrouded was he, as it were a meede
90 Al ful of fresshe floures, whyte and reede.
Syngynge he was, or floytynge, al the day;
He was as fressh as is the month of May.
Short was his gowne, with sleves longe and wyde.
Wel koude he sitte on hors and faire ryde.
95 He koude songes make and wel endite,
Juste and eek daunce, and weel purtreye and write.

So hoote he lovede that by nyghtertale
He sleep namoore than dooth a nyghtyngale.
Curteis he was, lowely, and servysable,
100　And carf biforn his fader at the table.
　　A YEMAN hadde he and servantz namo
At that tyme, for hym liste ride so,
And he was clad in cote and hood of grene.
A sheef of pecok arwes, bright and kene,
105　Under his belt he bar ful thriftily
(Wel koude he dresse his takel yemanly;
His arwes drouped noght with fetheres lowe),
And in his hand he baar a myghty bowe.
A not heed hadde he, with a broun visage.
110　Of wodecraft wel koude he al the usage.
Upon his arm he baar a gay bracer,
And by his syde a swerd and a bokeler,
And on that oother syde a gay daggere
Harneised wel and sharp as point of spere;
115　A Cristopher on his brest of silver sheene.
An horn he bar, the bawdryk was of grene;
A forster was he, soothly, as I gese.
　　Ther was also a Nonne, a PRIORESSE,
That of hir smylyng was ful symple and coy;
120　Hire gretteste ooth was but by Seinte Loy;
And she was cleped madame Eglentyne.
Ful weel she soong the service dyvyne,
Entuned in hir nose ful semely;
And Frenssh she spak ful faire and fetisly,
125　After the scole of Stratford atte Bowe,
For Frenssh of Parys was to hire unknowe.
At mete wel ytaught was she with alle;
She leet no morsel from hir lippes falle,
Ne wette hir fyngres in hir sauce depe;
130　Wel koude she carie a morsel and wel kepe

That no drope ne fille upon hire brest.
In curteisie was set ful muchel hir lest.
Hir over-lippe wyped she so clene
That in hir coppe ther was no ferthyng sene
135 Of grece, whan she dronken hadde hir draughte.
Ful semely after hir mete she raughte.
And sikerly she was of greet desport,
And ful plesaunt, and amyable of port,
And peyned hire to countrefete cheere
140 Of court, and to been estatlich of manere,
And to ben holden digne of reverence.
But for to speken of hire conscience,
She was so charitable and so pitous
She wolde wepe, if that she saugh a mous
145 Kaught in a trappe, if it were deed or bledde.
Of smale houndes hadde she that she fedde
With rosted flessh, or milk and wastel-breed.
But soore wepte she if oon of hem were deed,
Or if men smoot it with a yerde smerte;
150 And al was conscience and tendre herte.
Ful semyly hir wympul pynched was,
Hir nose tretys, hir eyen greye as glas,
Hir mouth ful smal, and therto softe and reed.
But sikerly she hadde a fair forheed;
155 It was almoost a spanne brood, I trowe;
For, hardily, she was nat undergrowe.
Ful fetys was hir cloke, as I was war.
Of smal coral aboute hire arm she bar
A peire of bedes, gauded al with grene,
160 And theron heng a brooch of gold ful sheene,
On which ther was first write a crowned A,
And after *Amor vincit omnia.*

    Another NONNE with hire hadde she,
That was hir chapeleyne, and preestes thre.

165   A MONK ther was, a fair for the maistrie,
An outridere, that lovede venerie,
A manly man, to been an abbot able.
Ful many a deyntee hors hadde he in stable,
And whan he rood, men myghte his brydel heere
170   Gynglen in a whistlynge wynd als cleere
And eek as loude as dooth the chapel belle
Ther as this lord was kepere of the celle.
The reule of Seint Maure or of Seint Beneit—
By cause that it was old and somdel streit
175   This ilke Monk leet olde thynges pace,
And heeld after the newe world the space.
He yaf nat of that text a pulled hen,
That seith that hunters ben nat hooly men,
Ne that a monk, whan he is recchelees,
180   Is likned til a fissh that is waterlees—
This is to seyn, a monk out of his cloystre.
But thilke text heeld he nat worth an oystre;
And I seyde his opinion was good.
What sholde he studie and make hymselven wood,
185   Upon a book in cloystre alwey to poure,
Or swynken with his handes, and laboure,
As Austyn bit? How shal the world be served?
Lat Austyn have his swynk to hym reserved!
Therfore he was a prikasour aright:
190   Grehoundes he hadde as swift as fowel in flight;
Of prikyng and of huntyng for the hare
Was al his lust, for no cost wolde he spare.
I seigh his sleves purfiled at the hond
With grys, and that the fyneste of a lond;
195   And for to festne his hood under his chyn,
He hadde of gold ywroght a ful curious pyn;
A love-knotte in the gretter ende ther was.
His heed was balled, that shoon as any glas,

And eek his face, as he hadde been enoynt.
200   He was a lord ful fat and in good poynt;
His eyen stepe, and rollynge in his heed,
That stemed as a forneys of a leed;
His bootes souple, his hors in greet estaat.
Now certeinly he was a fair prelaat;
205   He was nat pale as a forpyned goost.
A fat swan loved he best of any roost.
His palfrey was as broun as is a berye.
　　　A FRERE ther was, a wantowne and a merye,
A lymytour, a ful solempne man.
210   In alle the ordres foure is noon that kan
So muchel of daliaunce and fair langage.
He hadde maad ful many a mariage
Of yonge wommen at his owene cost.
Unto his ordre he was a noble post.
215   Ful wel biloved and famulier was he
With frankeleyns over al in his contree,
And eek with worthy wommen of the toun;
For he hadde power of confessioun,
As seyde hymself, moore than a curat,
220   For of his ordre he was licenciat.
Ful swetely herde he confessioun,
And plesaunt was his absolucioun:
He was an esy man to yeve penaunce,
Ther as he wiste to have a good pitaunce.
225   For unto a povre ordre for to yive
Is signe that a man is wel yshryve;
For if he yaf, he dorste make avaunt,
He wiste that a man was repentaunt;
For many a man so hard is of his herte,
230   He may nat wepe, althogh hym soore smerte.
Therfore in stede of wepynge and preyeres
Men moote yeve silver to the povre freres.

His typet was ay farsed ful of knyves
And pynnes, for to yeven faire wyves.
235 And certeinly he hadde a murye note:
Wel koude he synge and pleyen on a rote;
Of yeddynges he baar outrely the pris.
His nekke whit was as the flour-de-lys;
Therto he strong was as a champioun.
240 He knew the tavernes wel in every toun
And everich hostiler and tappestere
Bet than a lazar or a beggestere,
For unto swich a worthy man as he
Acorded nat, as by his facultee,
245 To have with sike lazars aqueyntaunce.
It is nat honest; it may nat avaunce,
For to deelen with no swich poraille,
But al with riche and selleres of vitaille.
And over al, ther as profit sholde arise,
250 Curteis he was and lowely of servyse;
Ther nas no man nowher so vertuous.
He was the beste beggere in his hous;
252ᵃ [And yaf a certeyn ferme for the graunt;
252ᵇ Noon of his bretheren cam ther in his haunt;]
For thogh a wydwe hadde noght a sho,
So plesaunt was his '*In principio*',
255 Yet wolde he have a ferthyng, er he wente.
His purchas was wel bettre than his rente.
And rage he koude, as it were right a whelp.
In love-dayes ther koude he muchel help,
For ther he was nat lyk a cloysterer
260 With a thredbare cope, as is a povre scoler,
But he was lyk a maister or a pope.
Of double worstede was his semycope,
That rounded as a belle out of the presse.
Somwhat he lipsed, for his wantownesse,

265 To make his Englissh sweete upon his tonge;
And in his harpyng, whan that he hadde songe,
His eyen twynkled in his heed aryght
As doon the sterres in the frosty nyght.
This worthy lymytour was cleped Huberd.
270 A MARCHANT was ther with a forked berd,
In mottelee, and hye on horse he sat;
Upon his heed a Flaundryssh bever hat,
His bootes clasped faire and fetisly.
His resons he spak ful solempnely,
275 Sownynge alwey th'encrees of his wynnyng.
He wolde the see were kept for any thyng
Bitwixe Middelburgh and Orewelle.
Wel koude he in eschaunge sheeldes selle.
This worthy man ful wel his wit bisette:
280 Ther wiste no wight that he was in dette,
So estatly was he of his governaunce
With his bargaynes and with his chevyssaunce.
For sothe he was a worthy man with alle,
But, sooth to seyn, I noot how men hym calle.
285 A CLERK ther was of Oxenford also,
That unto logyk hadde longe ygo.
As leene was his hors as is a rake,
And he nas nat right fat, I undertake,
But looked holwe, and therto sobrely.
290 Ful thredbare was his overeste courtepy,
For he hadde geten hym yet no benefice,
Ne was so worldly for to have office.
For hym was levere have at his beddes heed
Twenty bookes, clad in blak or reed,
295 Of Aristotle and his philosophie
Than robes riche, or fithele, or gay sautrie.
But al be that he was a philosophre,
Yet hadde he but litel gold in cofre;

But al that he myghte of his freendes hente,
300 On bookes and on lernynge he it spente,
And bisily gan for the soules preye
Of hem that yaf hym wherwith to scoleye.
Of studie took he moost cure and moost heede.
Noght o word spak he moore than was neede,
305 And that was seyd in forme and reverence,
And short and quyk and ful of hy sentence;
Sownynge in moral vertu was his speche,
And gladly wolde he lerne and gladly teche.

   A SERGEANT OF THE LAWE, war and wys,
310 That often hadde been at the Parvys,
Ther was also, ful riche of excellence.
Discreet he was and of greet reverence—
He semed swich, his wordes weren so wise.
Justice he was ful often in assise,
315 By patente and by pleyn commissioun.
For his science and for his heigh renoun,
Of fees and robes hadde he many oon.
So greet a purchasour was nowher noon:
Al was fee symple to hym in effect;
320 His purchasyng myghte nat been infect.
Nowher so bisy a man as he ther nas,
And yet he semed bisier than he was.
In termes hadde he caas and doomes alle
That from the tyme of kyng William were falle.
325 Therto he koude endite and make a thyng,
Ther koude no wight pynche at his writyng;
And every statut koude he pleyn by rote.
He rood but hoomly in a medlee cote,
Girt with a ceint of silk, with barres smale;
330 Of his array telle I no lenger tale.

   A FRANKELEYN was in his compaignye.
Whit was his berd as is the dayesye;

Of his complexioun he was sangwyn.
Wel loved he by the morwe a sop in wyn;
335 To lyven in delit was evere his wone,
For he was Epicurus owene sone,
That heeld opinioun that pleyn delit
Was verray felicitee parfit.
An housholdere, and that a greet, was he;
340 Seint Julian he was in his contree.
His breed, his ale, was alweys after oon;
A bettre envyned man was nowher noon.
Withoute bake mete was nevere his hous,
Of fissh and flessh, and that so plentevous
345 It snewed in his hous of mete and drynke;
Of alle deyntees that men koude thynke,
After the sondry sesons of the yeer,
So chaunged he his mete and his soper.
Ful many a fat partrich hadde he in muwe,
350 And many a breem and many a luce in stuwe.
Wo was his cook but if his sauce were
Poynaunt and sharp, and redy al his geere.
His table dormant in his halle alway
Stood redy covered al the longe day.
355 At sessiouns ther was he lord and sire;
Ful ofte tyme he was knyght of the shire.
An anlaas and a gipser al of silk
Heeng at his girdel, whit as morne milk.
A shirreve hadde he been, and a contour.
360 Was nowher swich a worthy vavasour.
　　　An HABERDASSHERE and a CARPENTER,
A WEBBE, a DYERE, and a TAPYCER—
And they were clothed alle in o lyveree
Of a solempne and a greet fraternitee.
365 Ful fressh and newe hir geere apiked was;
Hir knyves were chaped noght with bras

But al with silver, wroght ful clene and weel,
Hire girdles and hir pouches everydeel.
Wel semed ech of hem a fair burgeys
370 To sitten in a yeldehalle on a deys.
Everich, for the wisdom that he kan,
Was shaply for to been an alderman.
For catel hadde they ynogh and rente,
And eek hir wyves wolde it wel assente;
375 And elles certeyn were they to blame.
It is ful fair to been ycleped 'madame',
And goon to vigilies al bifore,
And have a mantel roialliche ybore.

A COOK they hadde with hem for the nones
380 To boille the chiknes with the marybones,
And poudre-marchant tart and galyngale.
Wel koude he knowe a draughte of Londoun ale.
He koude rooste, and sethe, and broille, and frye,
Maken mortreux, and wel bake a pye.
385 But greet harm was it, as it thoughte me,
That on his shyne a mormal hadde he.
For blankmanger, that made he with the beste.

A SHIPMAN was ther, wonynge fer by weste;
For aught I woot, he was of Dertemouthe.
390 He rood upon a rouncy, as he kouthe,
In a gowne of faldyng to the knee.
A daggere hangynge on a laas hadde he
Aboute his nekke, under his arm adoun.
The hoote somer hadde maad his hewe al broun;
395 And certeinly he was a good felawe.
Ful many a draughte of wyn had he ydrawe
Fro Burdeux-ward, whil that the chapman sleep.
Of nyce conscience took he no keep.
If that he faught and hadde the hyer hond,
400 By water he sente hem hoom to every lond.

But of his craft to rekene wel his tydes,
His stremes, and his daungers hym bisides,
His herberwe, and his moone, his lodemenage,
Ther nas noon swich from Hulle to Cartage.

405 Hardy he was and wys to undertake;
With many a tempest hadde his berd been shake.
He knew alle the havenes, as they were,
Fro Gootlond to the cape of Fynystere,
And every cryke in Britaigne and in Spayne.

410 His barge ycleped was the Maudelayne.
    With us ther was a DOCTOUR OF PHISIK;
In al this world ne was ther noon hym lik,
To speke of phisik and of surgerye,
For he was grounded in astronomye.

415 He kepte his pacient a ful greet deel
In houres by his magyk natureel.
Wel koude he fortunen the ascendent
Of his ymages for his pacient.
He knew the cause of everich maladye,

420 Were it of hoot, or coold, or moyste, or drye,
And where they engendred, and of what humour.
He was a verray, parfit praktisour:
The cause yknowe, and of his harm the roote,
Anon he yaf the sike man his boote.

425 Ful redy hadde he his apothecaries
To sende hym drogges and his letuaries,
For ech of hem made oother for to wynne—
Hir frendshipe nas nat newe to bigynne.
Wel knew he the olde Esculapius,

430 And Deyscorides, and eek Rufus,
Olde Ypocras, Haly, and Galyen,
Serapion, Razis, and Avycen,
Averrois, Damascien, and Constantyn,
Bernard, and Gatesden, and Gilbertyn.

435   Of his diete mesurable was he,
       For it was of no superfluitee,
       But of greet norissyng and digestible.
       His studie was but litel on the Bible.
       In sangwyn and in pers he clad was al,
440   Lyned with taffata and with sendal.
       And yet he was but esy of dispence;
       He kepte that he wan in pestilence.
       For gold in phisik is a cordial,
       Therefore he lovede gold in special.

445   A good WIF was ther OF biside BATHE,
       But she was somdel deef, and that was scathe.
       Of clooth-makyng she hadde swich an haunt
       She passed hem of Ypres and of Gaunt.
       In al the parisshe wif ne was ther noon
450   That to the offrynge bifore hire sholde goon;
       And if ther dide, certeyn so wrooth was she
       That she was out of alle charitee.
       Hir coverchiefs ful fyne weren of ground;
       I dorste swere they weyeden ten pound
455   That on a Sonday weren upon hir heed.
       Hir hosen weren of fyn scarlet reed,
       Ful streite yteyd, and shoes ful moyste and newe.
       Boold was hir face, and fair, and reed of hewe.
       She was a worthy womman al hir lyve:
460   Housbondes at chirche dore she hadde fyve,
       Withouten oother compaignye in youthe—
       But thereof nedeth nat to speke as nowthe.
       And thries hadde she been at Jerusalem;
       She hadde passed many a straunge strem;
465   At Rome she hadde been, and at Boloigne,
       In Galice at Seint-Jame, and at Coloigne.
       She koude muchel of wandrynge by the weye.
       Gat-tothed was she, soothly for to seye.

Upon an amblere esily she sat,
470 Ywympled wel, and on hir heed an hat
As brood as is a bokeler or a targe;
A foot-mantel aboute hir hipes large,
And on hir feet a paire of spores sharpe.
In felaweshipe wel koude she laughe and carpe.
475 Of remedies of love she knew per chaunce,
For she koude of that art the olde daunce.
A good man was ther of religioun,
And was a povre PERSOUN OF A TOUN,
But riche he was of hooly thoght and werk.
480 He was also a lerned man, a clerk,
That Cristes gospel trewely wolde preche;
His parisshens devoutly wolde he teche.
Benygne he was, and wonder diligent,
And in adversitee ful pacient,
485 And swich he was ypreved ofte sithes.
Ful looth were hym to cursen for his tithes,
But rather wolde he yeven, out of doute,
Unto his povre parisshens aboute
Of his offryng and eek of his substaunce.
490 He koude in litel thyng have suffisaunce.
Wyd was his parisshe, and houses fer asonder,
But he ne lefte nat, for reyn ne thonder,
In siknesse nor in meschief to visite
The ferreste in his parisshe, muche and lite,
495 Upon his feet, and in his hand a staf.
This noble ensample to his sheep he yaf,
That first he wroghte, and afterward he taughte.
Out of the gospel he tho wordes caughte,
And this figure he added eek therto,
500 That if gold ruste, what shal iren do?
For if a preest be foul, on whom we truste,
No wonder is a lewed man to ruste;

And shame it is, if a prest take keep,
A shiten shepherde and a clene sheep.
505 Wel oghte a preest ensample for to yive,
By his clennesse, how that his sheep sholde lyve.
He sette nat his benefice to hyre
And leet his sheep encombred in the myre
And ran to Londoun unto Seinte Poules
510 To seken hym a chaunterie for soules,
Or with a bretherhed to been withholde;
But dwelte at hoom, and kepte wel his folde,
So that the wolf ne made it nat myscarie;
He was a shepherde and noght a mercenarie.
515 And though he hooly were and vertuous,
He was to synful men nat despitous,
Ne of his speche daungerous ne digne,
But in his techyng discreet and benygne.
To drawen folk to hevene by fairnesse,
520 By good ensample, this was his bisynesse.
But it were any persone obstinat,
What so he were, of heigh or lough estat,
Hym wolde he snybben sharply for the nonys.
A bettre preest I trowe that nowher noon ys.
525 He waited after no pompe and reverence,
Ne maked him a spiced conscience,
But Cristes loore and his apostles twelve
He taughte; but first he folwed it hymselve.
        With hym ther was a PLOWMAN, was his brother,
530 That hadde ylad of dong ful many a fother;
A trewe swynkere and a good was he,
Lyvynge in pees and parfit charitee.
God loved he best with al his hoole herte
At alle tymes, thogh him gamed or smerte,
535 And thanne his neighebor right as hymselve.
He wolde thresshe, and therto dyke and delve,

For Cristes sake, for every povre wight,
Withouten hire, if it lay in his myght.
His tithes payde he ful faire and wel,
540   Bothe of his propre swynk and his catel.
In a tabard he rood upon a mere.
    Ther was also a REVE, and a MILLERE,
A SOMNOUR, and a PARDONER also,
A MAUNCIPLE, and myself – ther were namo.
545   The MILLERE was a stout carl for the nones;
Ful byg he was of brawn, and eek of bones.
That proved wel, for over al ther he cam,
At wrastlynge he wolde have alwey the ram.
He was short-sholdred, brood, a thikke knarre;
550   Ther was no dore that he nolde heve of harre,
Or breke it at a rennyng with his heed.
His berd as any sowe or fox was reed,
And therto brood, as though it were a spade.
Upon the cop right of his nose he hade
555   A werte, and theron stood a toft of herys,
Reed as the brustles of a sowes erys;
His nosethirles blake were and wyde.
A swerd and a bokeler bar he by his syde.
His mouth as greet was as a greet forneys.
560   He was a janglere and a goliardeys,
And that was moost of synne and harlotries.
Wel koude he stelen corn and tollen thries;
And yet he hadde a thombe of gold, pardee.
A whit cote and a blew hood wered he.
565   A baggepipe wel koude he blowe and sowne,
And therwithal he broghte us out of towne.
    A gentil MAUNCIPLE was ther of a temple,
Of which achatours myghte take exemple
For to be wise in byynge of vitaille;
570   For wheither that he payde or took by taille,

Algate he wayted so in his achaat
That he was ay biforn and in good staat.
Now is nat that of God a ful fair grace
That swich a lewed mannes wit shal pace
575 The wisdom of an heep of lerned men?
Of maistres hadde he mo than thries ten,
That weren of lawe expert and curious,
Of which ther were a duszeyne in that hous
Worthy to been stywardes of rente and lond
580 Of any lord that is in Engelond,
To make hym lyve by his propre good
In honour dettelees (but if he were wood),
Or lyve as scarsly as hym list desire;
And able for to helpen al a shire
585 In any caas that myghte falle or happe.
And yet this Manciple sette hir aller cappe.
  The REVE was a sclendre colerik man.
His berd was shave as ny as ever he kan;
His heer was by his erys ful round yshorn;
590 His top was dokked lyk a preest biforn.
Ful longe were his legges and ful lene,
Ylyk a staf; ther was no calf ysene.
Wel koude he kepe a gerner and a bynne;
Ther was noon auditour koude on him wynne.
595 Wel wiste he by the droghte and by the reyn
The yeldynge of his seed and of his greyn.
His lordes sheep, his neet, his dayerye,
His swyn, his hors, his stoor, and his pultrye
Was hoolly in this Reves governynge,
600 And by his covenant yaf the rekenynge,
Syn that his lord was twenty yeer of age.
Ther koude no man brynge hym in arrerage.
Ther nas baillif, ne hierde, nor oother hyne,
That he ne knew his sleighte and his covyne;

605 They were adrad of hym as of the deeth.
His wonyng was ful faire upon an heeth;
With grene trees yshadwed was his place.
He koude bettre than his lord purchace.
Ful riche he was astored pryvely.

610 His lord wel koude he plesen subtilly,
To yeve and lene hym of his owene good,
And have a thank, and yet a cote and hood.
In youthe he hadde lerned a good myster:
He was a wel good wrighte, a carpenter.

615 This Reve sat upon a ful good stot
That was al pomely grey and highte Scot.
A long surcote of pers upon he hade,
And by his syde he baar a rusty blade.
Of Northfolk was this Reve of which I telle,

620 Biside a toun men clepen Baldeswelle.
Tukked he was as is a frere aboute,
And evere he rood the hyndreste of oure route.

A SOMONOUR was ther with us in that place,
That hadde a fyr-reed cherubynnes face,

625 For saucefleem he was, with eyen narwe.
As hoot he was and lecherous as a sparwe,
With scalled browes blake and piled berd.
Of his visage children were aferd.
Ther nas quyk-silver, lytarge, ne brymstoon,

630 Boras, ceruce, ne oille of tartre noon,
Ne oynement that wolde clense and byte,
That hym myghte helpen of his whelkes white,
Nor of the knobbes sittynge on his chekes.
Wel loved he garleek, oynons, and eek lekes,

635 And for to drynken strong wyn, reed as blood;
Thanne wolde he speke and crie as he were wood.
And whan that he wel dronken hadde the wyn,
Thanne wolde he speke no word but Latyn.

A fewe termes hadde he, two or thre,
640 That he had lerned out of som decree—
No wonder is, he herde it al the day;
And eek ye knowen wel how that a jay
Kan clepen 'Watte' as wel as kan the pope.
But whoso koude in oother thyng hym grope,
645 Thanne hadde he spent al his philosophie;
Ay 'Questio quid iuris' wolde he crie.
He was a gentil harlot and a kynde;
A bettre felawe sholde men noght fynde.
He wolde suffre for a quart of wyn
650 A good felawe to have his concubyn
A twelf month, and excuse hym atte fulle;
Ful prively a fynch eek koude he pulle.
And if he foond owher a good felawe,
He wolde techen him to have noon awe
655 In swich caas of the ercedekenes curs,
But if a mannes soule were in his purs;
For in his purs he sholde ypunysshed be.
'Purs is the ercedekenes helle,' seyde he.
But wel I woot he lyed right in dede;
660 Of cursyng oghte ech gilty man him drede,
For curs wol slee right as assoillyng savith,
And also war hym of a *Significavit*.
In daunger hadde he at his owene gise
The yonge girles of the diocise,
665 And knew hir conseil, and was al hir reed.
A gerland hadde he set upon his heed,
As greet as it were for an ale-stake.
A bokeleer hadde he maad hym of a cake.
   With hym ther rood a gentil PARDONER
670 Of Rouncivale, his freend and his compeer,
That streight was comen fro the court of Rome.
Ful loude he soong 'Com hider, love, to me!'

This Somonour bar to hym a stif burdoun;
Was nevere trompe of half so greet a soun.
675 This Pardoner hadde heer as yelow as wex,
But smothe it heeng as dooth a strike of flex;
By ounces henge his lokkes that he hadde,
And therwith he his shuldres overspradde;
But thynne it lay, by colpons oon and oon.
680 But hood, for jolitee, wered he noon,
For it was trussed up in his walet.
Hym thoughte he rood al of the newe jet;
Dischevelee, save his cappe, he rood al bare.
Swiche glarynge eyen hadde he as an hare.
685 A vernycle hadde he sowed upon his cappe.
His walet, biforn hym in his lappe,
Bretful of pardoun comen from Rome al hoot.
A voys he hadde as smal as hath a goot.
No berd hadde he, ne nevere sholde have;
690 As smothe it was as it were late shave.
I trowe he were a geldyng or a mare.
But of his craft, fro Berwyk into Ware
Ne was ther swich another pardoner.
For in his male he hadde a pilwe-beer,
695 Which that he seyde was Oure Lady veyl;
He seyde he hadde a gobet of the seyl
That Seint Peter hadde, whan that he wente
Upon the see, til Jhesu Crist hym hente.
He hadde a croys of latoun ful of stones,
700 And in a glas he hadde pigges bones.
But with thise relikes, whan that he fond
A povre person dwellynge upon lond,
Upon a day he gat hym moore moneye
Than that the person gat in monthes tweye;
705 And thus, with feyned flaterye and japes,
He made the person and the peple his apes.

But trewely to tellen atte laste,
He was in chirche a noble ecclesiaste.
Wel koude he rede a lessoun or a storie,
710 But alderbest he song an offertorie;
For wel he wiste, whan that song was songe,
He moste preche and wel affile his tonge
To wynne silver, as he ful wel koude;
Therefore he song the murierly and loude.
715   Now have I toold you soothly, in a clause,
Th'estaat, th'array, the nombre, and eek the cause
Why that assembled was this compaignye
In Southwerk at this gentil hostelrye
That highte the Tabard, faste by the Belle.
720 But now is tyme to yow for to telle
How that we baren us that ilke nyght,
Whan we were in that hostelrie alyght;
And after wol I telle of our viage
And al the remenaunt of oure pilgrimage.
725 But first I pray yow, of youre curteisye,
That ye n'arette it nat my vileynye,
Thogh that I pleynly speke in this mateere,
To telle yow hir wordes and hir cheere,
Ne thogh I speke hir wordes proprely.
730 For this ye knowen al so wel as I:
Whoso shal telle a tale after a man,
He moot reherce as ny as evere he kan
Everich a word, if it be in his charge,
Al speke he never so rudeliche and large,
735 Or ellis he moot telle his tale untrewe,
Or feyne thyng, or fynde wordes newe.
He may nat spare, althogh he were his brother;
He moot as wel seye o word as another.
Crist spak hymself ful brode in hooly writ,
740 And wel ye woot no vileynye is it.

Eek Plato seith, whoso kan hym rede,
The wordes moote be cosyn to the dede.
Also I prey yow to foryeve it me,
Al have I nat set folk in hir degree
745   Heere in this tale, as that they sholde stonde.
My wit is short, ye may wel understonde.
    Greet chiere made oure Hoost us everichon,
And to the soper sette he us anon.
He served us with vitaille at the beste;
750   Strong was the wyn, and wel to drynke us leste.
A semely man OURE HOOSTE was withalle
For to been a marchal in an halle.
A large man he was with eyen stepe—
A fairer burgeys was ther noon in Chepe—
755   Boold of his speche, and wys, and wel ytaught,
And of manhod hym lakkede right naught.
Eek therto he was right a myrie man;
And after soper pleyen he bigan,
And spak of myrthe amonges othere thynges,
760   Whan that we hadde maad oure rekenynges,
And seyde thus: 'Now, lordynges, trewely,
Ye been to me right welcome, hertely;
For by my trouthe, if that I shal nat lye,
I saugh nat this yeer so myrie a compaignye
765   Atones in this herberwe as is now.
Fayn wolde I doon yow myrthe, wiste I how.
And of a myrthe I am right now bythoght,
To doon yow ese, and it shal coste noght.
    'Ye goon to Caunterbury – God yow speede,
770   The blisful martir quite yow youre meede!
And wel I woot, as ye goon by the weye,
Ye shapen yow to talen and to pleye;
For trewely, confort ne myrthe is noon
To ride by the weye doumb as a stoon;

23

775 And therfore wol I maken yow disport,
As I seyde erst, and doon yow som confort.
And if yow liketh alle by oon assent
For to stonden at my juggement,
And for to werken as I shal yow seye,

780 Tomorwe, whan ye riden by the weye,
Now, by my fader soule that is deed,
But ye be myrie, I wol yeve yow myn heed!
Hoold up youre hondes, withouten moore speche.'
   Oure conseil was nat longe for to seche.

785 Us thoughte it was noght worth to make it wys,
And graunted hym withouten moore avys,
And bad him seye his voirdit as hym leste.
'Lordynges,' quod he, 'now herkneth for the beste;
But taak it nought, I prey yow, in desdeyn.

790 This is the poynt, to speken short and pleyn,
That ech of yow, to shorte with oure weye,
In this viage shal telle tales tweye
To Caunterbury-ward, I mene it so,
And homward he shal tellen othere two,

795 Of aventures that whilom han bifalle.
And which of yow that bereth hym best of alle—
That is to seyn, that telleth in this caas
Tales of best sentence and moost solaas—
Shal have a soper at oure aller cost

800 Heere in this place, sittynge by this post,
Whan that we come agayn fro Caunterbury.
And for to make yow the moore mury,
I wol myselven goodly with yow ryde,
Right at myn owene cost, and be youre gyde;

805 And whoso wole my juggement withseye
Shal paye al that we spenden by the weye.
And if ye vouche sauf that it be so,
Tel me anon, withouten wordes mo,

And I wol erly shape me therfore.'
810   This thyng was graunted, and oure othes swore
With ful glad herte, and preyden hym also
That he wolde vouche sauf for to do so,
And that he wolde been oure governour,
And of oure tales juge and reportour,
815   And sette a soper at a certeyn pris,
And we wol reuled been at his devys
In heigh and lough; and thus by oon assent
We been acorded to his juggement.
And therupon the wyn was fet anon;
820   We dronken, and to reste wente echon,
Withouten any lenger taryynge.

        Amorwe, whan that day bigan to sprynge,
Up roos oure Hoost, and was oure aller cok,
And gadrede us togidre alle in a flok,
825   And forth we riden a litel moore than paas
Unto the Wateryng of Seint Thomas;
And there oure Hoost bigan his hors areste
And seyde, 'Lordynges, herkneth, if yow leste.
Ye woot youre foreward, and I it yow recorde.
830   If even-song and morwe-song accorde,
Lat se now who shal telle the firste tale.
As evere mote I drynke wyn or ale,
Whoso be rebel to my juggement
Shal paye for al that by the wey is spent.
835   Now draweth cut, er that we ferrer twynne;
He which that hath the shorteste shal bigynne.
Sire Knyght,' quod he, 'my mayster and my lord,
Now draweth cut, for that is myn accord.
Cometh neer,' quod he, 'my lady Prioresse.
840   And ye, sire Clerk, lat be youre shamefastnesse,
Ne studieth noght; ley hond to, every man!'
Anon to drawen every wight bigan,

And shortly for to tellen as it was,
Were it by aventure, or sort, or cas,
845 The sothe is this: the cut fil to the Knyght,
Of which ful blithe and glad was every wyght,
And telle he moste his tale, as was resoun,
By foreward and by composicioun,
As ye han herd; what nedeth wordes mo?
850 And whan this goode man saugh that it was so,
As he that wys was and obedient
To kepe his foreward by his free assent,
He seyde, 'Syn I shal bigynne the game,
What, welcome be the cut, a Goddes name!
855 Now lat us ryde, and herkneth what I seye.'
And with that word we ryden forth oure weye,
And he bigan with right a myrie cheere
His tale anon, and seyde as ye may heere.

Notes

The Canterbury Tales is a collection of stories told by a group of narrators. This was a familiar way of organizing a book in the late Fourteenth century. For example, Boccaccio's Italian prose work the *Decameron*, composed between 1348 and 1353, relates the hundred stories told by ten young people of noble birth during the ten days they stayed at a villa outside Florence in order to escape the plague of 1348. But Chaucer is original in his choice of setting, a pilgrimage – a journey to Canterbury to pray at the shrine of St Thomas à Becket. Such collections of stories normally began by describing the circumstances in which the storytellers came together, but Chaucer adds elaborate portrayals of each pilgrim. By describing so many people he offers a portrait of the society in which he lived, in the tradition of Medieval Estates Satire. (See Approaches p. 82 and Jill Mann, *Chaucer and Medieval Estates Satire*.)

The *General Prologue* begins by describing the season and Chaucer's meeting with the other pilgrims, continues with the individual descriptions of them, and concludes by setting out the terms of the competition in which the tales are to be told. Throughout the *General Prologue* the reader is invited to ask questions, to see implications and to evaluate the reliability and perceptiveness of the narrator figure, one of the pilgrims who is called 'Chaucer', but who seems to be more naive and less skilled than the author of *The Canterbury Tales*. (See Approaches pp. 79–80, 115–18.)

Another issue which it is best to raise at the outset, since you will be involved with it throughout, is Chaucer's use of irony. Irony is saying one thing and meaning another. Typically someone might use words which praise in order to condemn. For example someone might say 'well done', when I spill the tea on the floor. In normal conversation we might call this sarcasm, and recognize it as a form of verbal abuse which is especially enjoyable for onlookers and especially wounding for the victim. Writers often use irony to amuse audiences and to attack people or practices. The difficulty is to decide from a written text when a term of praise is meant seriously and when it is meant ironically. In conversation we can usually tell from the tone of voice employed. In reading a text we have to look for evidence of a mismatch between the language employed and the view presented. So that whether or not a particular expression is taken as ironic may depend on a person's own opinion about one of the pilgrims. Some people think that the words of praise which Chaucer applies to The Knight are intended ironically, others take them at face value. Sometimes new historical discoveries can alter our judgements of irony. For example, people used to think that it was an affectation for The Prioress to sing mass through her nose (122–3). This made them read many of the positive words applied to her as ironic. Putting these ironies alongside her other shortcomings, they regarded the whole portrait as a bitter denunciation. In the 1940s it was discovered that some medieval books recommend a nasal delivery in order to rest the voice. This weakened the case for interpreting Chaucer's words ironically and opened the possibility of a more positive reading of The Prioress.

The Opening: Lines 1–18

Long poems often begin with long sentences, as if to proclaim the poet's skill at the outset. In his opening sentence Chaucer brings together many different ideas and sensations within a structure which remains clear and unforced. The sentence seems to move through four phases. It begins with nature: the rain water making the earth fruitful, and the air breathing life into the fields, as if the world is being created anew. Then it turns to generation, with the growth of the plants in spring and the courtship songs and matings of the birds. Next it speaks of humans who are moved to travel great distances on pilgrimage in the spring, because the roads are now passable, and because spring rekindles the love of God, as much as earthly love. Finally the focus narrows to England, where people travel particularly to the shrine of St Thomas, renowned for its miracles of healing. Do you think that this sentence reconciles these natural, human and supernatural aspects of spring? Or are there tensions between, say, the awakening of sexual love and the religious urge to go on pilgrimages? Can you think of other tensions in the sentence?

This sentence is full of realistic detail (the April showers [1], the plants [4], the birds [9], the pilgrims [12]) as if Chaucer were writing the literary equivalent of the paintings of 'labours of the months' in medieval books of hours. (See illustration for April on p. 128.) But critics have also pointed to the way in which it exploits literary tradition, particularly the tradition of the springtime opening of the medieval dream-vision. Compare this passage with those printed in the Appendix (pp. 149–50). (See also Approaches pp. 87–8.)

2 **droghte of March**   Is March usually a dry month in Britain? Or is this a literary convention (based perhaps on poems written in Italy or Greece)?

2–3 **to the roote... every veyne**   literally the roots and veins belong to plants which will produce the flowers (4). Grammatically they also belong to the drought and by association to the earth.

3–4 **swich licour... flour**   liquid by whose power the flower is brought into being. The sense is that the rising of the sap promotes new growth and initiates the reproductive cycle of the plant.

5 **Zephirus**   the mild west wind, envisaged in classical mythology as a god.

6 **Inspired**   breathed life into.

7 **croppes**   shoots.

8 **Ram... yronne**   a much debated problem, though not a very important one. Prior to the reform of the calendar (1582 in most Catholic countries, 1752 in Britain) the sun was in Aries (*the Ram*) roughly between 11 March and 11 April. Halfway through Aries would therefore be about March 25, which would contradict line 1. So Walter Skeat in his 1890 edition of *The Canterbury Tales* suggests that the sun had completed the *second* half of Aries, which brings the date to 11 or 12 April. This would fit in reasonably well with 16 or 17 April, the dates implied for *The Parson's Tale*, which is delivered a few days after Chaucer meets the pilgrims. But both these dates are difficult to reconcile with 18 April, mentioned as the date of *The Sergeant of the Law's Tale*. Perhaps Chaucer would have sorted out this confusion if he had lived to revise the whole poem for publication. The sun is *yonge* (7) because Aries is the first sign of the solar new year, beginning at the spring equinox.

10 **open ye** Chaucer may be alluding to the belief that the nightingale sings continuously for fifteen days in the mating season. (See also line 98.)

11 **So... corages** so nature spurs them in their desires. Literally *corage* means 'heart' or 'spirit', but it often carries a sexual connotation. Could there be something ironic or subversive about Chaucer's decision to rhyme *corages* with *pilgrimages* (12)?

13 **palmeres** pilgrims who carried a palm leaf as a sign that they had visited the Holy Land.

straunge strondes foreign shores.

17 **blisful martir** blessed martyr, St Thomas à Becket, Archbishop of Canterbury, who was murdered by followers of Henry II in his cathedral on 29 December 1170. Becket's shrine had a reputation for miraculous healing. Hence it was much visited and richly decorated with gold and jewels. The idea here is that the pilgrims are visiting the shrine not to be healed, but to give thanks to the saint for his intercession in helping them overcome sickness in the past.

Lines 19–42

Where the first sentence evokes the large context of spring and pilgrimage, the second brings us firmly down to local reality, with Chaucer taking a night's lodging at a real and rather well-appointed inn, the Tabard in Southwark. Southwark at this time was a small town at the south end of London Bridge, outside the jurisdiction of the city of London. Pilgrims often lodged in Southwark prior to setting out on the road to Canterbury. It was quite usual for travellers to band together for protection against the dangers of the road.

Chaucer sets the pilgrimage story in motion and then immediately suspends it in order to describe his fellow pilgrims.

What is your first impression of Chaucer, the narrator of the poem? (See Approaches pp. 78–80, 115–18.)

19–26 This sentence is analysed in A Note on Chaucer's English, p. 135.

22 **with ful devout corage** in a very pious spirit.

24 **nyne and twenty** the *General Prologue* mentions thirty pilgrims (including the three priests who accompany The Prioress, but excluding Chaucer and the innkeeper, Harry Baily).

Perhaps Chaucer intended twenty-nine so that when he joined he would bring the number in the story-telling competition to thirty, or perhaps he miscounted.

29 **And... beste**   And we were certainly made very comfortable.

33 **forward**   agreement.

37 **Me... resoun**   It seems to me logical.

38–41 Chaucer here indicates that he will describe the circumstances (*condicioun* [38]), occupation (*whiche they weren* [40]), social rank (*degree* [40]) and dress (*array* [41]) of the pilgrims. How far do Chaucer's descriptions fit in with the pattern he offers here?

42 Many different theories have been advanced about the order of the portraits. Jill Mann in her book, *Chaucer and Medieval Estates Satire* points out that Chaucer avoids the usual order of Medieval Estates Satire (first clergy, then laity, then women). Michael Alexander in *Prologue to The Canterbury Tales* (p. 54) suggests the following scheme:

1	Military	Knight, Squire, Yeoman
2	Clergy	Prioress, Monk, Friar
3	Bourgeois	Merchant, Clerk, Sergeant of the Law, Franklin, Five Guildsmen, Cook, Shipman, Doctor of Physic, Wife of Bath
4	Good men	Parson, Ploughman
5	Petty Bourgeois	Miller, Manciple, Reeve
6	Church Officers	Summoner, Pardoner

Can you point out any inconsistencies in this scheme? (It may not be easy to think of a better one.) Perhaps the order is pragmatic, as though Chaucer started by placing together people who are related (as individuals or as a social group). When this became predictable, he varied it by putting contrasting characters together. Sometimes he uses the ordering to point out similarities we might not have suspected. For further discussion of the order see Approaches pp. 80, 90–2.

The Knight

Knights were soldiers who fought on horseback. They held lands in return for military service to their feudal overlords, the barons. In the feudal system, the King theoretically owned all the land in his realm. He granted control over large tracts of land to the great lords of the realm in return for service, financial and military, and loyalty. The great lords granted lands to lesser lords on similar terms. In the same way the lesser lords granted lands to the knights. This meant, firstly that everyone apart from the King owed service to a superior, and secondly, that a well organized army could be raised from the land when it was required. Knights rented part of their lands out to farmers in return for produce or services. Local inhabitants, both freemen and serfs, were obliged to devote part of their time to working on the knight's estate. Peasant farmers only held land from him as tenants and he was responsible for the administration of law within his territory. Usually the eldest son of a knight would inherit all his father's lands, leaving the younger sons with the necessity of making their own way economically, through marriage (in that the bride's father would give property to the couple) or through service to their elder brother or another feudal lord. Chaucer's description of The Knight makes no reference to his lands (though perhaps the presence of The Yeoman indicates that he had some) or to his administrative responsibilities. Perhaps he neglected them or perhaps he was a younger son.

Chaucer describes The Knight's values, his campaigns, his behaviour and his appearance. Other aspects of knightly life (love, hunting) appear in the portraits of The Squire and The Yeoman. Do the many approving adjectives (e.g. *worthy* used five times) support the traditional view that The Knight is an ideal figure beside who the others can be judged or should we take them ironically? Whereas most English soldiers of his time would have fought in France, The Knight's campaigns in Spain, Morocco, Turkey and the Baltic states were all crusades. Terry Jones in *Chaucer's Knight* has suggested that these particular campaigns were disreputable and that Chaucer meant us to regard The Knight as a mercenary. Maurice Keen ('Chaucer's Knight, the English Aristocracy and the Crusade'), in reply, pointed to evidence of the prestige of crusading among late fourteenth century English aristocrats. Some of them took part for religious reasons, others for personal glory, but fighting in France was more lucrative. What do you think Chaucer tells us about The Knight's motives? What is the significance of his plain, rust-stained clothes?

45–6 These five qualities summarize the ideals of knightly behaviour: skill in fighting (*chivalrie*), loyalty and honesty (*trouthe*), honourable behaviour, generosity (*fredom*), and good manners and consideration for others (*curteisie*). (See Approaches pp. 93–4.)

47 Probably the reference is to The Knight's feudal overlord, but it could mean God, in which case *therto* (48) would mean 'for that purpose'.

48 **therto** in addition.

ferre farther.

49 **hethenesse** non-Christian countries.

51–67 The places and the battles Chaucer mentions fall into four groups. Algeciras (*Algezir* [57]) in the kingdom of Granada (*Gernade* [56]), part of Spain, was captured from the Muslims in 1344. A raid on Morocco (*Belmarye* [57]) may have been connected with this campaign. King Peter of Cyprus led campaigns against the Muslims in the near East. He attacked Antalya (*Satalye* [58]) in Turkey in 1361, Alexandria (*Alisaundre* [51]) in Egypt in 1365 and Ayash (*Lyeys* [58]) in modern Lebanon in 1367. The independent Muslim prince of Balat (*Palatye* [65]) in Turkey made peace with Peter in 1365. The Teutonic knights (a religious order of German knights and priests, founded in 1189) made raids (*reysed* [54]) from Prussia (*Pruce* [53]) into Lithuania (*Lettow* [54]) and Russia (*Ruce* [54]) throughout the second half of the Fourteenth century. They aimed to settle parts of the modern Baltic republics under Christian control. There is no record of a Christian attack on Tlemcen (*Tramyssene* [62]) in Algeria in the Fourteenth century. Terry Jones (*Chaucer's Knight*) suggests that The Knight fought for a Muslim prince there. Do you think that the context (*for oure feith* [62]) will allow this? Jill Mann (*Chaucer and Medieval Estates Satire*) says that lists of campaigns often appear in courtly descriptions, to demonstrate the worth of a knight and to evoke the romance of distant countries. What should we make of the disorder of this list of campaigns?

52 He had sat in the place of honour at the head of the table. The Teutonic knights sometimes held feasts to honour the deeds of knights who had come to their aid.

54 **reysed** ridden on raids.

59 **Grete See**   Mediterranean Sea.

63 **lystes**   literally the arena erected for a tournament, here 'formal duels', presumably fought by representatives from the opposing armies.

67 **everemoore**   always.

sovereyn prys   pre-eminent reputation.

69 **port**   behaviour, manner.

meeke   humble, submissive. Is The Knight's exceptionally modest behaviour and speech a sign of virtue, or is it difficult to believe?

70 **vileynye**   rude words, vulgarity. Literally the language (or the behaviour) appropriate to a *villein*, someone low born. In Middle English words connected with high birth (*gentil, fre*) are associated with virtuous and admirable behaviour, while words denoting low birth acquire negative meanings. How much does this linguistic bias in favour of the well born continue into Modern English? (Consider the use of words like 'noble' or 'common'.)

71 **no maner wight**   any sort of person.

72 **verray**   true.

parfit   perfect.

gentil   noble, gracious. Are we to think that this comment is justified? Is it meant ironically? Or is the naïve approval of Chaucer the pilgrim undercut by the factual detail of the portrait?

74 **gay**   richly clothed.

75 **fustian**   coarse cloth.

gypon   tunic.

76 Stained (with rust) from his coat of chain-mail (*habergeon*).

The Squire

A squire was a young male member of the knightly class who was preparing to become a knight, learning the customs of his order by serving an established knight. Chaucer's Squire performs the relatively menial task of carving his father's meat. His fighting experience is different from his father's and so are his interests. The Squire has many of the accomplishments expected of a young courtier and some aspects of the description (and the language in which it is couched) are conventional. Some critics have found The Squire's devotion to love excessive while others have praised him for his youthful vitality and his artistic inclinations. What do you think the contrasts between father and son mean?

80 **lusty** lively.
    bacheler bachelor; the degree of knighthood which The Squire has attained rather than 'unmarried man'. (Compare with Bachelor of Arts.)

81 **crulle** curled.
    presse press, curler.

83 **evene lengthe** moderate height.

84 **delyvere** active, agile.

85 **somtyme** once.
    in chyvachie on a cavalry expedition.

86 Flanders, Artois and Picardy are districts of northern France (now partly in Belgium) where Chaucer himself served in the army in his youth.

87 **born hym** conducted himself.
    space time.

88 **stonden in his lady grace** win the favour of his lady. The Squire goes to war to show off his skill and impress his lady.

89 **Embrouded** (his clothes were) embroidered.
    meede meadow.

91 **floytynge** playing the flute.

92 **fressh** youthful, blooming, vigorous.

93 Should we admire The Squire's elegant, fashionable clothes, or is some criticism intended? See illustration of The Squire from the Ellesmere manuscript on p. 129.

94–6 Knights were expected to be skilful riders. Dancing, writing music and poetry, and jousting were considered suitable accomplishments for aristocratic young men. *Purtreye* (96) may mean 'describe' rather than 'draw' because courtiers were not usually taught drawing.

97 **by nyghtertale** at night time. (see line 10.)

99 **lowely** modest.
    servysable attentive, willing to serve. It is to The Squire's credit that he serves his father willingly and gracefully.

The Yeoman

A yeoman was a free servant (i.e. not a serf as many of the agricultural workers were), above the grooms but below the squire in a feudal household. By profession The Yeoman is a forester, a gamekeeper, but here he serves as The Knight's bodyguard. (See lines 111–14). There was no tradition of describing foresters in Estates Satire. Chaucer concentrates on The Yeoman's appearance and the tools of his trade.

101 **namo** no more. Why does The Knight (*he*) not have a larger retinue?

102 **hym liste** he preferred to.

104 Peacock feathers were (and are) used in making good quality arrows.

    kene sharp.

105 **bar ful thriftily** carried very carefully.

106 **dresse** care for, prepare.

    takel tackle, equipment.

    yemanly skilfully, as a yeoman should.

107 Feathers which did not stand out properly (*fetheres lowe*) would cause an arrow to fall short (*droupe*).

109 **not heed** a close cropped head. The Yeoman's face is brown (*broun*) from exposure to sun, wind and rain.

110 He understood all the customs and practices of woodcraft.

    In this period woodcraft may refer particularly to gamekeeping and hunting.

111 **gay bracer** bright armguard.

112 **bokeler** small shield.

114 **Harneised** mounted, ornamented.

115 **Cristopher** a medallion of St Christopher, patron saint of travellers.

    sheene bright.

116 **bawdryk** baldric, shoulderstrap. What is the effect of the portrait of The Yeoman? Does Chaucer include it to amplify his portrayal of The Knight, to remind us that commoners fought alongside nobles, or to extend his picture of the activities of the land?

The Prioress

The Prioress, first of the group of ecclesiastical figures is one of only two women described in the *General Prologue* (The Wife of Bath is the other). What might this imply? The interpretation of the portrait has been much fought over in relation to debates about the nature of Chaucer's irony.

Two fundamental points seem to be agreed: that the external details of the portrait (her name [121], her table manners [127–36], her social behaviour [137–41] and her appearance [151–4, 157–62]) imitate the descriptions of heroines in romances and that many of her actions are unsuited to a nun. For example nuns were forbidden to go on pilgrimages, to keep dogs and to wear fashionable clothes. There are also faults of omission. One might expect that the description of a nun would say more about her religious life and about her concern for the sufferings of other humans. Some critics (such as James Winny, in his Cambridge edition of the *General Prologue*) see Chaucer's underlying purpose as satirical, to expose the gulf between her charming and complacent social exterior and the true obligations of her calling. But there are other ways of interpreting the difference between Chaucer's portrait and our expectations about nuns. For E. T. Donaldson (*Chaucer's Poetry*), Chaucer the pilgrim is so overwhelmed by the charm of The Prioress that his naïve and inappropriate praise reveals his infatuation more than it establishes her excellence. Derek Pearsall (*The Canterbury Tales*), on the other hand, insists that the mildness of The Prioress's failings forces the reader to 'feel that his urge to disapprove is unduly harsh'. For him the portrait makes a strict moral judgement of The Prioress impossible. Jill Mann (*Chaucer and Medieval Estates Satire*) has shown that some medieval writers identified a spiritual courtliness appropriate to the nun as the beloved of Christ, though she concludes that The Prioress's *curteisie* (132) is wordly rather than spiritual. We should also remember that although the *General Prologue* says nothing about her religious convictions, the prologue to her tale is a prayer. The tale itself combines a simple Christian piety with a streak of violent anti-semitism.

The portrait also raises questions about the relationship between literature and historical reality. The expenses involved in arranging marriages at the higher social levels meant that many younger daughters of noble families found themselves in The Prioress's position, caught between two codes. Brought up in a courtly atmosphere, they could find themselves at the age of fifteen or sixteen forced into a religious life for which they felt little real vocation. Eileen Power, in a chapter on Madame Eglentyne in her pioneering social history, *Medieval People*, has shown that many of The Prioress's failings reflect the reality of fourteenth century convent life as revealed in visitation records (records of the regular inspections of monasteries and convents carried out by the local bishop). Eileen Power in *Medieval People* quotes a Lincoln visitation of 1436 in which the nuns complain that their prioress wears:

> golden rings exceeding costly, with divers precious stones and also girdles silvered and gilded over and silken veils and she carries her veil too high above her forehead, so that her forehead, being entirely uncovered, can be seen of all, and she wears furs of vair (a type of squirrel). Also she wears shifts of cloth of Rennes, which costs sixteen pence the ell (about 115 cm). Also she wears kirtles laced with silk and tiring pins of silver and silver gilt and has made all the nuns wear the like ... Item she has on her neck a long silken band, in English a lace, which hangs down below her breast and thereon a golden ring with one diamond. (p. 85)

119 **symple and coy** innocent and quiet. These two adjectives are often found together in descriptions of courtly heroines. *Coy* implies shyness but not coquettishness. How do you think we should interpret Chaucer's decision to begin his description of a nun by talking about her smile?

120 **ooth** Strictly speaking a prioress should neither swear nor go on pilgrimages, but if her strongest oath is such a mild one it is unlikely that much criticism is intended.
  Seinte Loy is St Eligius (588–629) by trade a goldsmith. He was renowned for his beauty and courtliness.

122 **Eglentyne** literally 'briar rose' but also a name found in romances. Nuns choose a new name when they make their vows. Would you draw conclusions from The Prioress's choice of this name rather than one associated with a virtue or a religious figure? (See Approaches p. 111.)

123 **Intoned** with nasal delivery very elegantly. The possible ironies

of language are very carefully balanced. *Ful semely* (123) and *ful weel* (122) could be ironic, but since they describe her skill in singing the mass they might well be meant seriously. Nasal delivery was not an affectation but a way of taking strain off the voice. What do you make of Chaucer's rather frequent use of the intensifier *ful* (very) in this passage?

124–6   Speaking French was an important courtly skill. Even though French was no longer the language of government (as it had been from the Norman Conquest until the early Fourteenth century) it was still the language of culture and law. English poets of the time, such as Chaucer's friend John Gower wrote in French and Latin as well as in English.

    Some scholars take The Prioress's very elegant (*ful faire and fetisly* [124]) French literally, arguing that the nuns at St Leonard's convent in Stratford at Bow spoke a good version of Anglo-Norman French, as opposed to the Parisian French spoken at court and at a nearby convent at Barking. Others assume that the phrase is ironic and that Chaucer is making a joke about her Essex French. Which view seems more likely to you? Would Chaucer's position be inconsistent if he was criticizing The Prioress's over-courtly manners (127–41) at the same time as looking down on the quality of her French?

129–31   Forks were not in common use in England until the Sixteenth century, so polite eating required a certain manual dexterity (as it still does in some countries). Do Chaucer's remarks suggest that The Prioress was excessively interested in the etiquette of eating or merely that she had mastered an important skill? Why does he not talk about the table manners of other pilgrims? There is also a literary joke here. Chaucer is translating directly from a passage in the Old French poem the *Roman de la Rose* (c. 1275) in which La Vieille advises a young woman about how to attract men. (See Approaches p. 108 and Appendix p. 150).

132   She took the greatest pleasure in good manners.

133   **over-lippe**   upper lip.

134   **ferthyng**   drop, literally a farthing, a small round coin worth a quarter of an old penny.

136   'She reached for her food very graciously.' What is the effect of using so many words which indicate approval (*wel, ful semely, ful plesaunt*)?

137   **of greet desport**   very merry.

138   **amyable of port**   friendly in her manner.

139–40   **countrefete cheere/Of court**   to imitate the behaviour of the court.

141   **to ben holden digne**   to be considered worthy.

142–5   What do you think it means that Chaucer speaks of her *conscience* and her feelings of charity and pity in relation to a mouse caught in a trap rather than in relation to other cases which might require compassion? Compare the use of *conscience* and *tendre herte* in line 150.

147   **wastel-breed** was the most expensive bread generally available. Meat was usually too expensive to feed to dogs. What is Chaucer saying when he suggests that The Prioress's dogs ate better than most people? Eileen Power in her book, *Medieval People*, quotes a Winchester visitation of 1387 which complains about the animals (birds, hounds and rabbits) which the nuns bring into church with them, noting that the hunting dogs in the convent were eating the food which ought to be given to the poor, and fouling the cloisters.

150   **conscience**   solicitude, pity.

151   **wympul**   wimple, garment covering the whole head apart from the face (like a balaclava).
       pynched   pleated.

152–6   The well-formed (*tretys*) nose, the grey eyes and the small mouth were typical of the romance heroine, as was this type of part by part description (sometimes called a 'blazon'). But The Prioress's forehead may be too wide (though a certain breadth was a sign of beauty) and *she was nat undergrowe* may well be an understatement to indicate that she was very large. Might these lines explain why she became a nun rather than a nobleman's wife?

158–9   A nun ought to carry a rosary (a string of beads used to remember a sequence of prayers), but should it be as colourful as this one? The *gauds*, large beads representing *The Lord's Prayer*, are placed after every ten of the smaller beads, each of which represents *Hail Mary*, a shorter prayer addressed to St Mary, mother of Jesus Christ.

160–1   Nuns were not supposed to wear brooches. A crowned 'A' was a contemporary symbol for Queen Anne, wife of Richard II. How might these 'facts' influence your interpretation of Chaucer's view of The Prioress? What meaning does Chaucer convey by making the brooch hang from (*theron*) the rosary?

162 **Amor vincit omnia** (Latin) Love conquers all things. Do you think this refers to human love (appropriate to the would-be heroine of a romance) or to love of God (appropriate to the nun)? John Livingston Lowes comments in *Convention and Revolt in Poetry*, *Which of the two loves does 'Amor' mean to the Prioress? I do not know; but I think she thought she meant love celestial.*

163 The presence of a secretary (*chapeleyne* [164]) and three priests confirms the high status of The Prioress.

The Monk

Monks made vows to remove themselves from the world and devote themselves to prayer and contemplation. They lived in regulated communities, monasteries, which were usually situated at a distance from towns, or in remote places. Monasteries were often centres of religious devotion, learning and culture, but when they became wealthy, through agriculture or the gifts of local people, they could offer a life of easy self-indulgence. The long history of Christian monasticism (from the Fourth century AD to the present) is marked by successive waves of reform, attempts to renew the ideal of selfless devotion to prayer.

Chaucer's Monk loves hunting, good food and fine clothes. (See Approaches pp. 104–5.) He regards the rules of his order as old-fashioned and rather strict (174). Some critics think that Chaucer's attitude to The Monk is basically friendly, his satire gentle at most, where others treat the apparent approval (183) as bitterly ironic. Some recent critics detect The Monk's own voice in the amusing replies to those who criticize monks for breaking the rules. Jill Mann (*Chaucer and Medieval Estates Satire*) shows that Chaucer's description of The Monk's failings reflects traditions of anti-clerical satire. She argues that Chaucer omits the moral condemnation which would be usual in his sources. Must it be wrong for a monk to devote so much time to hunting and eating well? Or is he a charming man whose vices harm no one but himself?

165 **a... maistrie**   a good one, surpassing the others.

166 **outridere**   a monk with business outside the monastery (most monks were confined within the monastery walls).

venerie   hunting (sometimes used in the sense of pursuing love).

167 Does Chaucer mean that The Monk is worldly (or sexually active?) and seeking to become head of his monastery, or merely that he is companionable and may go far? Would this Monk really make a good abbot, or does he just think he would? Or is Chaucer implying that abbots are often as worldly as his Monk?

171 What effect does Chaucer achieve by comparing the jingling of the bells on his bridle to the sound of a chapel bell?

172 The Monk is in charge (*kepere*) of a small house (*celle*) of monks separate from the main monastery. Does Chaucer call him a lord because he remembers that monks often have the title *Dom* (short for *dominus* (Latin) meaning 'lord') or because he wants to convey something about this Monk's manner?

173 St Benedict (*Beneit*), c.480–c.547, drew up a rule which established Christian monasticism in Western Europe. His disciple St Maurus (*Maure*) is said to have brought the rule to France. What is Chaucer's attitude to The Monk's dismissal of the rule in the next few lines?

176 And followed the fashion of the modern world.

177 **pulled**   plucked. A plucked hen and an oyster were both of little value, but they suggest that The Monk measures things according to his love of food. Scholars argue about which *text* Chaucer refers to here.

179 **recchelees**   careless (about keeping the rules).

183 Does Chaucer agree with The Monk, or is his apparent approval an ironic way of highlighting the outrageousness of what The Monk says?

184–7 Monks were supposed to study and work (*swynken* [186]) with their hands.

187 **Austyn**   St Augustine of Hippo, 354–430, one of the greatest bishops and writers (e.g. *Confessions, City of God, On Christian Doctrine*) of the early Christian church, was reputed to have written a monastic rule.

bit   commands. Should The Monk be concerned with serving the world? Is Chaucer agreeing that observing the rule is futile, or are we here hearing the complacent voice of The Monk himself? Might this be a place where we should distinguish the approval of Chaucer the pilgrim from the irony of Chaucer the poet?

189 **prikasour** horseman, hunter. Why *Therfore*?

191 **prikyng** tracking (perhaps with a sexual innuendo).

193 His sleeves are lined (*purfiled*) at the wrist with the expensive fur (*grys* [194]) of the squirrel.

196 **curious** skilfully made.

197 **love-knotte** a knot or bow-shaped decoration.
gretter larger.
Love-knotte might describe only the shape of the pin, or it might indicate its significance. Monks should not have expensive ornaments or (still less) love-tokens.

200 **poynt** condition.

201 **stepe** prominent.

202 'Gleamed like a fire under a cauldron.' Does Chaucer admire The Monk's physique and his twinkling eyes or is he criticizing his overindulgence in food and drink?

203 **greet estaat** fine condition.

204 **prelaat** prelate, high-ranking churchman.

205 **forpyned goost** tormented spirit.

206 Roast swan was very expensive. James Winny in his Cambridge edition of *The General Prologue* (p. 96) suggests that while The Monk was a complete failure in his profession, Chaucer admired his vitality and his joyful response to life. Do you agree? How is the sense of The Monk's vitality conveyed?

The Friar

The orders of friars were founded in the late Thirteenth century by St Dominic, 1170–1221, and St Francis of Assisi, 1181–1226. Friars tended to be well-educated (many of the most famous theologians and philosophers of the Thirteenth and Fourteenth centuries were friars) and friaries were established in towns and near universities. Individual friars were supposed to have no possessions and to live by begging from the people they served (hence they were called mendic-ants), but friaries soon became rich from the gifts of wealthy people. The most splendid churches in most Italian cities belong to the Franciscans and the Dominicans. The parish clergy, who tended to lose out in the competition for gifts and legacies, often accused the friars of cultivating the rich and giving them easy penances. Estates Satire echoes these complaints.

Chaucer emphasizes his Friar's smooth talk, his involvement with women, his fine dress and the profits he makes from the abuse of confession (218–32). These characteristics conflict with his vows of poverty, chastity and obedience, but he is not the avaricious lecher sometimes found in satire against friars (see Jill Mann, *Chaucer and Medieval Estates Satire*, pp. 40–1) nor even a greedy hypocrite like the friar in *The Summoner's Tale*. On a strictly religious reading both he and The Monk corrupt the ideals of their calling. Which do you think has the more serious faults, and why? Is Chaucer's judgement influenced by considerations of personal attractiveness? The Appendix (p. 151) contains a discussion of friars from William Langland's *Piers Plowman*. You may find it interesting to compare it with Chaucer's.

208 **wantowne** jolly, pleasure-loving (sometimes with a sexual implication).
209 A limiter (*lymytour*) is a friar licensed by his order to beg within a particular area.
   solempne dignified.
210 There were four orders of friars: Dominicans, Franciscans, Carmelites and Augustinians.
   kan knows.
211 **daliaunce** sociable talk (sometimes 'flirting').
212–13 Paying dowries to enable poor women to marry was regarded as a religious act of charity, but here the implication may be that The Friar is compensating women he has seduced.
214 What is the implication of this remark (and of the rhyme)?
216 **frankeleyns** landowners. (See line 331.)
219 **curat** parish priest. Sometimes friars were given special duties connected with confession, but *As seyde hymself* may imply that The Friar is making false claims to attract clients.
220 Whereas all parish priests could hear confession only those friars who were licensed (*licenciat*) by their order could do so.
221 On absolution and penance see Notes to The Pardoner (pp. 69–70). That The Friar heard confessions in a kindly manner (*swetely*) and was lenient (*esy* [223]) in giving penance

may suit someone at the time of confession but may endanger the soul later (i.e. if the sinner is not fully contrite, or if he or she repeats the offence). Friars were often accused of becoming rich through the gratitude of those whose souls they had put at risk through their leniency, as if, in their hands, confession ceased to be a way of saving souls and became a way of making money.

224 **Ther** where.

pitaunce donation.

226 **wel yshryve** well confessed, truly sorry.

227 If a man gave, he (The Friar) dared to assert...

230 **hym soore smerte** he suffers painfully. Is his acceptance of payment kindly and realistic or hypocritical and self-serving?

232 Friars were meant to be poor (*povre*) but in practice they often were not. Chaucer's Friar needed a substantial income to pay for marriages (212), presents (233–4), tavern bills (240) and fine clothes (261–2). (See Approaches pp. 104–5.)

233 **typet** dangling point of the hood.

farsed stuffed.

235–7 What do you make of The Friar's skill at secular music?

236 **rote** stringed instrument.

237 **yeddynges** songs. (Compare with line 266.)

baar outrely the pris absolutely took the prize.

238 **flour-de-lys** lily.

239 A champion represented someone else in a trial by combat.

241 **hostiler** innkeeper.

tappestere barmaid.

242 **lazar** leper.

beggestere beggar woman.

244 **facultee** professional dignity. What are we to make of Chaucer applying the words *worthy* (243) and *honest* (246) (honourable) to The Friar's refusal to associate with the poor and the sick?

246–7 **it may ... poraille** there is no profit in dealing with such poor people.

248 **But al** but only.

vitaille victuals, food.

249 **over al** above all.

ther as where.

250 **lowely of servyse** humble in bearing. Compare his conduct among the wealthy to his attitude to the poor and the sick.

251 How are we to take *vertuous* here?

252 a-b The Friar paid a fee (*ferme*) for the right (*graunt*) to beg in his usual district (*haunt*). These lines appear in only a few manuscripts. It has been suggested that Chaucer withdrew them because they are inaccurate. No English limiter is known to have paid a fee in return for exclusive rights in his territory.

253 **sho**   shoe (i.e. she was extremely poor).

254 '*In principio*'   is Latin for 'In the beginning' (the first words of the Gospel according to John).

255 **ferthyng**   see line 134.

256 A proverbial phrase implying excess profits. In this case probably his personal income (*purchas*) exceeded what he passed on to his friary (*rente*), but it could mean (following on from 252a) that the income he made from his district exceeded what he paid for exclusive rights.

257 **rage**   sport, frolic (sometimes with a sexual implication).
  whelp   puppy.

258 **love-dayes**   days on which disputes were resolved.

259 **cloysterer**   monk.

260 A *cope* was a long cloak, the outer garment worn by monks and friars, sometimes seen as the distinctive mark of learned or church men. Compare The Friar's clothes with those of The Monk and The Clerk.

261 **maister**   master of arts.

262 **double worstede**   thick, expensive cloth.
  semycope   short cope. See note to line 260.

263 Round, like a bell fresh from its mould.

264 **lipsed**   lisped.
  wantownesse   affectation.

267–8 What is the effect of this sudden and vivid comparison?

269 **cleped**   called.

The Merchant

Chaucer turns from the higher ranking ecclesiastical pilgrims to a group of secular figures associated with business, learning and the professions. The Merchant seems to be a large-scale businessman, involved in export (probably of cloth) and in the currency deals needed to finance exports. Chaucer only hints at the nature of the deals, which may suggest a reticence on the part of The Merchant.

He describes The Merchant's appearance, conversation, and manner, hinting that he is much less prosperous than he seems. In this he differs from contemporary Estates Satire which tends to accuse merchants of avarice and excessive wealth. It is an understated portrait, suggesting a pompous man, with something to hide.

Chaucer may have known a lot about merchants, from his family background and from his work in the Custom House, but apart from the rather elusive reference to *sheeldes* (278) he avoids the display of technical knowledge which appears in his portraits of The Sergeant of the Law and The Doctor of Physic. There is evidence, particularly in Langland's poem, *Piers Plowman,* that contemporaries were troubled by the emergence of large-scale merchants.

270 **forked berd**   a beard divided into two parts. Portraits show that Chaucer himself followed this fashion. Is he making a joke by giving a devious character his own shape of beard?

271–3 **mottelee**   cloth of mixed colour, like a tweed. The Merchant's clothes, his expensive beaver-fur hat from Flanders and his boots elegantly (*fetisly*) clasped   suggest wealth or the need to make a good first impression. (See Approaches p. 98).

274 **solcmpnely**   gravely, perhaps pompously.

275 **Sownynge**   associated with sound, especially musical sound. So it could mean that The Merchant is always talking about the money he makes or that the reasons he gives are always 'in accord with' the increase of his own profits.

276–7 He wanted the trading route between the ports of Middleburg, in the Netherlands, and Orwell, in Suffolk, kept open at all costs. Middleburg was the continental base of both associations of English merchants from 1384. Why should this be the main topic of The Merchant's political conversation?

278 **sheeld(es)**   the English translation of écu, either a unit of French currency or (more likely in this context) a Flemish 'money of account'. It used to be thought that The Merchant's currency dealings were illegal. The modern view is more complicated. The Merchant is selling in London bonds which he or his agents will have to redeem at a higher rate in Bruges. He obtains pounds to pay his present debts in England. By selling these bonds he is in effect borrowing money which he will have to repay in Bruges when he has sold his next shipment. This would be a legal way of managing a shortage of cash but in

the medieval view it is morally dubious (in that it is equivalent to paying interest). It also looks like a rather desperate move, mortgaging future profits in order to settle current debts.

279 **bisette** used.

281 **estatly** dignified.

governaunce behaviour.

282 **bargaynes** deals (sales and purchases).

chevyssaunce borrowing. (See Approaches p. 98).

283–4 What are we to make of Chaucer's repetition of *worthy*, and of his saying that he does not know (*noot* = *ne woot*) his name?

The Clerk

The Clerk is a poor scholar, who is pursuing his studies at Oxford University. Since he has been studying for a long time, and since Chaucer mentions that he has not yet obtained a church job (*benefice* [291]) presumably he is a priest. Why does Chaucer place him after The Merchant rather than before? Or why is he not beside the virtuous Parson? Perhaps Chaucer wanted to contrast his threadbare poverty with the wealth and pretension of the pilgrims on either side. Or perhaps placing him among the secular pilgrims fits in with the direction of his studies.

Chaucer's portrait concentrates on his poverty and his devotion to learning. His speech is brief, formal and moral. This contrasts with the students we meet in medieval satire and elsewhere in *The Canterbury Tales* (for example in *The Miller's Tale* and *The Reeve's Tale*), who are often boisterous, witty and lecherous. He is far less worldly than the other pilgrims, spending whatever money he has on books, which were very expensive in the fourteenth century. Do you think there may be some criticism of him as a 'perpetual student'? Or might we expect him to show more interest in Christian literature or in the religious duties he will take up when he finishes studying? At one point he suggests that his tale should be read as a religious allegory, but there are equally powerful indications that it is a human story about marriage.

286 'Who had been studying logic a long time before.' By the Fourteenth century logic was the most important subject in the

Bachelor of Arts degree, the first degree taken by all students. The skills taught in logic were used in the disputations and lectures which were required of those who wished to obtain higher degrees. Bachelors and Masters of Arts were also required to teach logic to undergraduates. Hence The Clerk still uses or teaches logic, even though he has moved on to higher studies.

289 **therto** also.

sobrely serious.

290 **overeste** uppermost.

courtepy jacket.

292 **office** secular job. Some priests took administrative posts in the service of great landowners.

293 **hym was levere** he would rather.

295 The works of the Greek philosopher Aristotle (384–322 BC) formed the basis of the arts course at medieval universities. The Clerk would have studied his books on logic, physics, biology, metaphysics, psychology and ethics. Twenty books (294) was a large private library. Books did not become really plentiful until printing (invented in the West c.1450) took over from manuscript copying towards the end of the Fifteenth century.

296 **fithele** fiddle.

gay sautrie elegant psaltery (a stringed instrument, like a small harp).

297–8 Chaucer puns on two medieval meanings of 'philosopher': the advanced student of arts who has not yet moved on to theology, medicine or law (the three higher faculties in the medieval university system) and the alchemist, one who seeks the 'philosopher's stone' which will transmute base metal into gold.

299 **hente** obtain. Does Chaucer criticize The Clerk for spending other people's money on books, or does his willingness to teach others save him from the charge of selfishness?

301 **bisily** earnestly.

gan... preye prayed.

302 **scoleye** attend university.

304 **o** one.

305 **in forme and reverence** with formality and respect.

306 **quyk** vivid.

hy sentence serious meaning.

307 **Sownynge** agreeing with, tending to. (See line 275.)

The Sergeant of the Law

Sergeants were a special group of very well-educated lawyers who had the exclusive right to plead in the Court of Common Pleas (one of the two highest courts in the land, the other being the King's Bench) and from whose ranks the judges were chosen. Usually they came from wealthy families. Chaucer emphasizes the Sergeant's knowledge of the law, his dignified appearance and his wealth.

What is the effect of Chaucer's use of the world *semed* (313, 322) meaning 'seemed'? Some critics see the portrait as strongly satirical, but Jill Mann (*Chaucer and Medieval Estates Satire*) points out that Chaucer avoids the complaints about the lawyer's greed and dishonesty found in Estates Satire. What conclusions do you draw from the portrait's emphasis on learning, honour and wealth, or from its lack of reference to justice?

- 310 **Parvys** probably the porch of St Paul's Cathedral, where clients consulted sergeants (or perhaps the porch of Westminster Hall, the seat of the courts).
- 311 **excellence** exceptional talent.
- 312 **Discreet** judicious.
  reverence dignity.
- 315 **patente** letter of appointment from the King.
  pleyn commissioun full jurisdiction.
- 316 **science** knowledge.
  heigh renoun great reputation.
- 317 **fees and robes** annual payments from wealthy men to secure access to his services. What effect does Chaucer achieve by including so much legal terminology in the portrait?
- 318 **purchasour** land buyer. Does *greet* mean that he bought a lot, or that he was very good at it?
- 319 **fee symple** absolute possession; the clearest and most profitable form of land ownership.
- 320 **infect** be invalidated. The Sergeant was good at converting difficult leases and other complicated ownership arrangements into the advantageous condition of *fee symple* (319).
- 322 Why might he want to seem busier than he was?
- 323 **termes** law reports.
  caas cases.
  doomes judgements.

325 **endite** draw up.
326 **pynche at** find an error in. It has been suggested that this word
  refers to Thomas Pinchbeck, a sergeant whom Chaucer may
  well have known.
327 And he knew every statute completely by heart.
329 **Girt** encircled.
  ceint belt.
  barres stripes.

The Franklin

Helen Cooper in her Oxford Guide reports that The Franklin causes
the fiercest debate over any of the pilgrims. He *can be made to seem
either the backbone of the social fabric or a man in the grip of deadly sin, a
glutton, proud and uncharitable* (p.45). See illustration of The Franklin
from the Ellesmere manuscript on p. 129.

A franklin was a 'free' (*franc*) man, a landowner without the military obligations of The Knight, who ranked above him. Chaucer's
Franklin owns a good deal of land (339) and has held important
judicial, political and administrative posts (355–9). The portrait
links his careful pursuit of these duties with another characteristic of
the English gentry: lavish feasting. Important men were expected to
provide abundant hospitality and this was one way in which wealthy
men from classes below the aristocracy could outshine their social
superiors. How much is The Franklin's interest in food attractive?
How much is it sinful? What are we to make of the ill-temper which
this apparently gracious man can show towards his cook (351)?

331 Why do The Franklin and The Sergeant ride together? Is it
  because they have interests in common, or might they be
  striking some deal which will benefit them both?
332 How does the simile influence our view of The Franklin?
333 **complexioun** temperament. According to the medieval view
  the body contained four fluids or humours (blood, phlegm,
  yellow bile and black bile). The excess of one of these humours
  could lead to disease; the relative preponderance of one could
  dictate traits of character. Four types of character were recognized (sanguine, phlegmatic, choleric and melancholic) of
  which the sanguine (*sangwyn*) was considered the most happy.

Although medicine has abandoned the theory of the four humours we still use these adjectives to describe character. (See also lines 420 and 587).

334 A piece of bread (*sop*) in wine was a common breakfast.

335 **delit** delight, pleasure.

wone custom.

336 Epicurus (341–270 BC) was a Greek philosopher who thought that pleasure was the highest purpose of life. For him the moral pleasures (such as friendship, or doing good to others) outweighed other kinds, but in the Middle Ages he was misrepresented as advocating unrestrained enjoyment of personal physical pleasure.

337–8 **pleyn delit... parfit** pure pleasure was true perfect happiness.

340 Julian the Hospitaller was the (legendary) patron saint of innkeepers.

341 **after oon** of uniformly good quality.

342 **envyned** stocked with wine.

345 How does this metaphor affect our view of The Franklin?

347 **After** according to.

sondry various. Seasonal change of diet was considered to be a good way of keeping the humours (333) in balance and thus of remaining healthy.

349 **muwe** pen for birds.

350 **breem** freshwater bream.

luce pike.

stuwe fish pond.

352 **Poynaunt** sharp, spicy.

geere cutlery.

353 His table was left permanently in place (*dormant*) in the hall, the main public room of his house. Since tables were usually taken down after meals (so that the hall could be used for other purposes) this observation confirms that food was The Franklin's top priority.

355–6 He presided at law courts (*sessiouns*), presumably as a Justice of the Peace, and represented his county in Parliament. Chaucer himself undertook both these responsibilities on occasion.

357 **anlaas** dagger.

gipser purse.

359 He had served his county both as sheriff, chief officer of the crown, and as *contour*, overseer of the collection of taxes.

360 **vavasour** (sub-vassal) is a technical term for the lowest rank of the nobility. Chaucer may mean that The Franklin surpassed the local nobility or that he had crossed the barrier into the higher class. In the late Fourteenth century people could be awarded noble (*gentil*) status in return for service to the crown, as happened to Chaucer's own family.

The Five Guildsmen

The Five Guildsmen represent the growing economic importance of shopkeepers and small manufacturers. The poll tax of 1379 assessed aldermen at the same rate as barons, merchants with knights. The wealth of Chaucer's Guildsmen entitles them to a leading position in the religious confraternity (364) whose ceremonial livery they wear. Why does Chaucer treat all five of them together? Do you think he satirizes their pride or pays tribute to their prominent role in society? What does he think of their wives (374–8)?

361 **Haberdasshere** haberdasher; seller of hats, caps and small items connected with dress, such as thread and tape.

362 **Webbe** weaver.

Tapycer weaver of tapestries and rugs.

364 **fraternitee** religious organization for lay people. Confraternities (or guilds) maintained chapels, and arranged burials, masses for the dead, and material social benefits. They also performed charitable works, for the benefit of their members' souls, including paying for schools. Some guilds united those who practised one particular trade, which the guild would control (e.g. by establishing standards of workmanship and regulating apprenticeships and admission to the trade). Such guilds were the forerunners of modern day employers' organizations and trades unions.

365 **geere** equipment.

apiked trimmed.

366 **chaped** mounted. The silver ornaments on their knives, belts and purses indicate a display of wealth and status. Such ornaments were forbidden to merchants and citizens unless they possessed property to the value of five hundred pounds.

367 **clene** brightly, splendidly.

369 **burgeys** burgess, member of the city council. The guildhall

(*yeldehalle* [370]) is the seat of the city government whose officials would sit on the dais (*deys* [370]).

371–2 Does Chaucer say that The Guildsmen possess (*kan*) the wisdom fitting (*shaply*) for aldermen, the highest ranking city officials, or do we hear the voices of The Guildsmen's own ambitions? Is Chaucer looking down on them from his higher social position?

373 **catel** goods, property.
rente income.

375 Is Chaucer confirming The Guildsmen's right to become aldermen, or do we hear the voices of their wives urging them on? Or is the phrase ironic?

376 Aldermen's wives were entitled to be called (*ycleped*) 'madam'.

377 **vigilies** vigils, religious services and feasts held on the eve of a saint's day.
bifore in front (of the procession). (Compare with line 450.)

378 **mantel** cloak.
roialliche ybore carried, like royalty.

The Cook

Estates Satire did not provide Chaucer with any models to draw on in portraying The Cook. The list of dishes and techniques seems to indicate his appreciation of The Cook's skill. But what does he think of his ulcer, probably (in the medieval view) the result of intemperate or unhygienic habits? Why does he mention The Cook's knowledge of London ale? In the prologue to his unfinished tale we learn that The Cook's name is Roger, that he originally came from Ware in Hertfordshire, and that he now has a shop in London. The Host accuses him of selling pies which have been reheated twice.

379 **for the nones** for the occasion. This Cook is not regularly employed by any of The Guildsmen. He is an independent businessman who has hired himself out to them for the duration of the pilgrimage. What does their hiring of The Cook tell us about The Guildsmen's attitude to their pilgrimage?

381 **poudre-marchant tart** a sharp-flavoured spice.
galyngale a root used in flavouring.

383 **sethe** simmer.

384 **mortreux** thick soup or stew.

385 **harm** pity.

as it thoughte me   as it seemed to me.
386 **shyne**   shin.
mormal   ulcer, running sore. (See Approaches p. 79.)
What is the effect of prefacing this observation with an expression of pity? Or of placing these lines at this point in the portrait?
387 **blankmanger**   a mousse made of chopped chicken (or fish) with rice.

The Shipman

The Shipman is a thief (396–7) and a murderer (400). His face is weatherbeaten (394) and he lacks the grace of a good horseman (390). But he is brave, experienced and skilful at navigation (401 –5). He knows all the harbours of north west Europe (407). Does Chaucer condemn the good captain for being a bad man? Is his vice unavoidable? Or is his skill so rare and necessary as to outweigh his crimes? Because Chaucer specifies that The Shipman sails the *Magdalen* (*Maudelayne* [410]) out of Dartmouth, scholars have tried to identify an original for this portrait (the current candidates are Piers Risselden and John Piers) but there is no general agreement.

390 **rouncy**   cart-horse.
as he kouthe   as best he could.
391 **faldyng**   coarse woollen cloth.
395 **felawe**   companion. Notice how Chaucer attaches this to what looks like drinking and turns out to be theft.
397 **Burdeux-ward**   from the direction of Bordeaux.
chapman   merchant (here the agent who accompanies the shipment).
398 **nyce**   scrupulous.
keep   notice.
400 He drowned the crew of the other vessel. This was a common way of disposing of the witnesses to piracy. What does this euphemism tell us about The Shipman? Would we expect Chaucer to condemn The Shipman's behaviour more strongly?
401–3 The Shipman is skilful at reckoning tides, currents and other hazards. He knows his harbours, the influence of the moon on tides, and how to pilot a ship (*lodemenage*). What is the relationship between this sentence and the previous one?

404 **Cartage** perhaps Cartagena in Spain rather than Carthage, in Tunisia, since, as far as we know, English captains did not sail the Mediterranean at this time.

405 **wys to undertake** prudent in his undertakings.

408 **Gootlond** is probably Gotland, an island off the Swedish coast, though it might be Jutland part of modern Denmark. Probably *Fynystere* is Cape Finisterre in northern Spain rather than Finistère in Brittany.

409 **cryke** creek, inlet.
   Britaigne Brittany.

410 **barge** a sea-going merchant vessel.

The Doctor of Physic

We are told that The Doctor of Physic has read the works of a large number of medical authorities (429–34) and that he understands all the methods of diagnosis and treatment favoured by his contemporaries (419–24). He is also well-dressed and miserly (439–41). Chaucer suggests that he receives commission from apothecaries (427) and hints at his atheism (438). But medieval satire usually treated doctors far more harshly than this, accusing them of deceitful incompetence, greed and lack of care for their patients. Do you see the portrait as critical or neutral? Can you think of anything positive in it? One would expect The Doctor to be placed beside The Sergeant or The Merchant. By associating him with The Shipman might Chaucer be making implications about The Doctor's morals or about his effect on his patients?

411–13 Chaucer's Doctor of Physic has the rare accomplishment of a doctorate in medicine. This necessitated many years of study on the continent. Surgery was often considered to be a separate and inferior skill, partly within the province of the barber.

413 **To speke of** in respect of, or perhaps 'for speaking of'.

414 Medical science was grounded in astronomy in the sense that the position of the stars when someone was born (their horoscope) would determine the balance of humours (see 333) within them. Equally by considering the position of the planets at the moment when a disease began the physician would work out which humour was in excess and when it would be most

propitious to intervene (by, for example, bloodletting or applying leeches) to draw off the humour which was in excess. In the Middle Ages the science of astronomy included what we now call astrology (and regard as superstition).

416 **houres**   may mean hours or stages or the disease, or astrological hours in which different planets had predominance.

magyk natureel   beneficent magic, involving co-operation with nature, as opposed to black magic, which involved calling up demons.

417 **fortunen the ascendent**   either calculate the position of the planets or position the planet coming over the horizon (*ascendent*) favourably for the patient. This refers to the practice of making talismans (*ymages* [418]) at auspicious moments. The talismans (and, in theory, the influence they preserved) would be applied to a part of the patient's body which was in need of help.

420 This line refers to the four humours (see lines 333 and 414): blood (hot and moist), phlegm (cold and moist), yellow bile (hot and dry) and black bile (cold and dry).

421 The excess of a particular humour originated (*engendred*) in a specific part of the body. Medieval physicians used elaborate tables which assigned parts of the body to particular humours and particular planets.

422 **praktisour**   practitioner. Is Chaucer's judgement here the same as in his parallel remark about The Knight (72)?

423 Once he knew the cause of the disease and the source of its ill effects.

424 **Anon**   at once.

boote   remedy, medication.

425 **apothecaries**   pharmacists.

426 **letuaries**   electuaries, medicines.

427 **wynne**   profit. What is the effect of linking the mention of remedies to the profitable collaboration of doctor and pharmacist?

429–34 Chaucer provides an extremely long list of medical authorities, among them: Aesculapius (*Esculapius*), the god who founded medicine according to Greek legend; Dioscorides Paedianus (*Deyscorides*), flourished in the first century AD, whose *Materia Medica* attempts to provide a systematic description of the medicines available to a doctor; Hippocrates (*Ypocras*), flourished

57

in the Fifth century BC, who used to be considered the author of the early Greek medical writings, the so-called *Hippocratic Corpus*; Rufus of Ephesus (*Rufus*); Galen (*Galyen*), 129–199 AD, Greek philosopher and author of the most influential ancient medical works; the Islamic medical authorities Ali ibn Abbas (*Haly*), died 994, and Rhazes (*Razis*), c. 854–930; the Islamic Aristotelian philosophers Avicenna (*Avycen*), 980–1037, and Averroes (*Averrois*), 1126–1198; Constantine the African (*Constantyn*), flourished 1065–1085, who translated medical works from Arabic; and some medieval English medical authorities, Bernard of Gordon (*Bernard*), flourished 1283–1309, John of Gaddesden (*Gatesden*), died around 1349, and Gilbertus Anglicus (*Gilbertyn*), flourished 1250. (The identity of *Serapion* is in dispute; Johannes Damascenus (*Damascien*) is given as the author of some medical books now known to have been written by others.) Why are there so many names? Is Chaucer poking fun at intellectual pedantry, or is he assuring us that this man really is a fine physician?

435 **mesurable** moderate.

436 **superfluitee** excess. Medieval authorities stress the influence of diet on health. Is The Doctor of Physic practising what he preaches or does he put his own health before his patients'?

438 What are the implications of The Doctor's limited Bible reading?

439 **sangwyn** red (with a pun on the humour).
pers grey-blue.

440 Taffeta and sendal were types of silk, which was expensive.

441 **but esy of dispence** only moderate in spending.

442 **wan** won, earned.
pestilence time of plague.

443 **cordial** medicine for the heart. Why does The Doctor of Physic especially like gold? (See Approaches p. 99.)

The Wife of Bath

Strictly *wif* means woman (as opposed to maiden) rather than wife, but Alison is so famous as The *Wife* of Bath that it would be pedantry to call her anything else. Chaucer's portrait concentrates on The Wife's sexuality, her trade, her extravagant clothing, her pride, her love of pilgrimages, and the effects of age on her. But these subjects are so intertwined that each reflects on the others and a composite impression animates all the separate details. Chaucer begins with her deafness (to elicit pity) but quickly moves on to ask us to admire the excellence of her weaving, and also to take pride in it since it surpasses the work of the weavers of Ypres and Ghent. In parallel to this, though we admire it less, there is her pride in her status within her own parish (and her determination to maintain it against the aspirations of other women). Her anger is commented on (and also softened) by the description of her absurd Sunday hats which weigh ten pounds. What is the effect of the rhyme which links the *worthy womman* (459) to the five husbands? What is the effect of Chaucer's use of the word *worthy* here? (Compare the way he uses it of The Knight (43) or The Merchant (279).) How does the audience react to the (*oother compaignye* [461]) which are not to be mentioned for now? Admiration, amusement, sympathy, outrage, broad laughter and mild censure succeed each other in this portrait. Satire against women contributes details to the portrait but the bitter effect of satire is absent from it. Anyone who wants to know more about The Wife's life and opinions will enjoy the long prologue to her tale. The portrait given here is consistent with that but different and independently delightful. (See Approaches pp. 110–14).

A medieval moralist might denounce her sins. Which of the seven deadly sins (pride, envy, lechery, anger, gluttony, avarice and sloth) do you think she is guilty of? Do you think Chaucer condemns her? Why does he mention her large hips, her laughter, her wide-set teeth, her deafness and details of her clothing'. See illustration of The Wife from the Ellesmere manuscript on p.129.

446 **somdel deef**   somewhat deaf.
     scathe   pity.
447 **haunt**   skill.
448 Flemish weavers, and especially those from Ypres and Ghent, were usually considered to be superior to British ones.
450 Worshippers used to go to the altar individually to present their offerings. Arguments about precedence were quite common.
452 When she is *out of alle charitee*, does charity denote the gift which she was about to present for the poor, the way she ought to treat her neighbours, or her love for God?

453 **coverchiefs** headcoverings.
    ground texture.
457 **streite yteyd** tightly laced.
    moyste supple.
461 **Withouten** not counting.
463–6 She has been to the most famous and most distant pilgrimage sites. At Jerusalem she would have seen the places associated with the death and resurrection of Christ, at Rome the chief basilicas of the city which commemorate the martyrdom of the leaders of the early Christian church (including St Peter and St Paul), at Boulogne an image of the virgin Mary, at Santiago di Compostella in Galicia (north-west Spain) the shrine of St James, and at Cologne the shrines of the three wise men and of St Ursula and the eleven thousand virgins said to have been martyred with her. Is Chaucer here poking fun at The Wife's excesses or emphasizing her extreme devotion, in making such long and expensive journeys? Or did she have other motives for going on pilgrimages? (See Approaches pp. 85, 88.)
464 **straunge strem** foreign river.
467 Does *wandrynge by the weye* refer to her experience of travel, or is there a (more critical) moral implication?
468 **Gat-tothed** her teeth were widely spaced. In her own prologue The Wife says that this facial feature fits in with her strong sexual desires. What is the effect of linking this line by rhyme to the *wandrynge* in the line above?
469 **amblere** ambling horse.
    esily comfortably.
470 A wimple covers the head and neck, leaving the face visible.
472 **foot-mantel** overskirt.
475 **love** i.e. lovesickness.
    per chaunce as it happened.
476 **koude** knew.
    olde daunce tricks of the trade.

The Parson

Chaucer emphasizes The Parson's strict fulfilment of the instructions of the gospel (481, 498, 527), his kindness to his parishioners (487, 518), and his devoted concern for them (492, 512). He must be an example as well as a guide (497). From Chaucer's discussion of what his Parson avoids we also learn a good deal about the vices prevalent among parish clergy (living far from the parish [509], corruption [507, 514], excessive concern with tithes [486]). Compare Chaucer's use of this material to William Langland's criticism of corrupt parish clergy in *Piers Plowman* (see Appendix p. 152). From time to time we seem to hear The Parson's own voice, making an analogy or drawing a lesson (499–506, 513, 519). Should The Parson's virtues be used to judge the other pilgrims? Or does the narrator's expression of approval for so many of the pilgrims (at least in their own terms) make it impossible for us to apply The Parson's standards to the others? Why does Chaucer place The Parson just after The Wife of Bath? See illustration from the Ellesmere manuscript on p. 129.

486 People were supposed to pay a tenth (*tithe*) of their income to support the parish priest and the church. The penalty for non-payment was excommunication, exclusion from the services of the Church and from the spiritual community of Christian souls. But Chaucer's Parson was very reluctant (*Ful looth*) to impose this penalty, which, if unrevoked, would result in the damnation (hence *cursen*) of the person involved.

489 From what the people gave him and from his church income.

490 He knew how to be content with little.

492 **lefte nat** did not omit.
    for in spite of.

494 **muche and lite** great and small.

499 **figure** figure of speech. The figures of speech were listed in the art of rhetoric, which was widely taught in medieval schools and universities. In the Middle Ages there was a special type of rhetoric textbook which taught the art of composing sermons.

502 **lewed man** uneducated man.

506 **clennesse** purity.

507–14 As a result of the Black Death (1349) the population of many parishes was reduced and the price of grain fell. This severely reduced the incomes of parish priests. Many responded by leaving their parishes to work for guilds (see 364) or landowners, singing masses for the souls of the dead or working as administrators.

507 **benefice** church job. Some priests would keep the income from a parish but hire someone else at a lower rate to perform the duties required.

509   In St Paul's Cathedral there were may chantries: jobs of singing masses for the souls of the dead. A rich person or a guild might provide money for this purpose since prayers and masses said on someone's behalf would help the soul pass through purgatory and on into heaven more rapidly.

511   To be employed by a confraternity (see 364).

514   **mercenarie**   hireling. The parson works out of a sense of responsibility and not merely for money. Commentators compare *John* 10, 12: *He that is an hireling, and not the shepherd, whose own the sheep are not, seeth the wolf coming, and leaveth the sheep and fleeth.* In the Latin *Bible*, the Vulgate, the equivalent for 'hireling' in this passage is *mercenarius*.

516   **despitous**   scornful.

517   **daungerous** and **digne**   both mean haughty, aloof.

519   **fairnesse**   gentle means.

520   **bisynesse**   endeavour.

521   **But**   unless, except.

523   **snybben**   rebuke.
       nonys   occasion, time.

525   **waited after**   expected.
       reverence   ceremony

526   **spiced**   over-particular. The priest did not give undue importance to minor sins, or did not worry about the technical details, but concentrated on essential Christian teaching.

The Ploughman

The Ploughman combines agricultural labour (the occupation of the vast majority of the population) with sincere religious devotion. He works hard out of duty as much as for his own advantage (531, 537). He follows Christ's two commandments (*Mark* 12, 30–1), loving God first, and then loving his neighbour as much as himself (533–5). The relationship between Parson and Ploughman reflects the ideal of a cohesive and religious society, in which people's conduct was based on a sense of unchanging obligations. (See Approaches pp. 100–1.) Commentators have pointed out that the relationship between The Ploughman and The Parson is very different from the relationships between other pilgrims. They have suggested that other alliances in the *General Prologue* are more short-term, entered into for mutual benefit, and dissoluble when those benefits disappear. Paul Strohm, in *Social Chaucer*, argues that this aspect of the *General Prologue* reflects a change in English society, from a structured and religious state based on eternal obligations towards a society based on short-term dissoluble contracts. (See Approaches p. 96).

530 **ylad** hauled.
   dong manure.
   fother cartload.
534 At all times, whether in pleasure or in pain.
536 **dyke** make ditches.
   delve dig.
539 That the ploughman paid tithes (486) indicates that he was a free man with a plot of land of his own. Most agricultural labourers were serfs. Critics have pointed out that the pilgrimage includes no representative of the highest ranks of society and no one from the lowest (the vast majority) either.
540 **propre swynk** own labour.
   catel property, possessions.
541 **mere** mare.
544 It is significant that Chaucer names himself among five rogues? Or might it be a conventional gesture of politeness, placing himself last?

The Miller

In contrast to the moral emphasis of the two preceding portraits, The Miller is described overwhelmingly in physical terms. He is strong and ugly, loud and foul-mouthed, and he cheats his customers. Can you find anything redeeming in this portrait? How would you compare The Miller with The Doctor of Physic or The Shipman? And yet The Miller tells one of the most delightful of all the tales, combining realistic description and a low view of human motivation with subtle and imaginative comedy. Perhaps Chaucer liked the bagpipes.

545 **stout carl** strong rogue; (*carl* has undertones of vice, like other words for the lower classes, such as churl or villain).
   for the nones indeed.
547 **over al ther he cam** wherever he went.

548 The ram would be the prize in the wrestling competition.

549 It is hard to reconcile *short-sholdred* with *brood* and *thikke*. Perhaps his forearms or his neck were short while his shoulders were broad. *Knarre* usually means 'crag', so perhaps 'rugged man'.

550 **nolde heve of harre** would not lift off its hinges.

552 What is the effect of comparing (parts of) The Miller to a sow (twice), a fox, a spade and an oven?

552–7 The medieval science of physiognomy aimed to determine people's character and morality on the basis of their faces. You can imagine how useful it would be to know what people are like just from looking at them! In the medieval manuals red hair and large nostrils (*nosethirles* [557]) were said to indicate anger, foolishness and lechery. A large mouth suggested gluttony and boldness. W. C. Curry has described the physiognomical implications of The Miller's face in detail in his *Chaucer and the Medieval Sciences*.

555 **werte** wart.

toft of herys tuft of hairs.

558 **bokeler** small shield.

bar carried, wore.

559 **forneys** oven, or perhaps cauldron.

560 **janglere** chatterer, teller of tales.

goliardeys buffoon, joker.

561 **harlotries** indecency.

562 **tollen thries** take three times the accepted payment. Farmers paid millers a proportion of the flour milled.

563 Millers judged grain with their thumbs, so a golden thumb might connect his profits with his skill. But there is also an allusion to the proverb: *an honest miller hath a golden thumb* which implies that there were no honest millers. (See Approaches p. 99.)

565 **sowne** play, sound.

The Manciple

A manciple's job was to purchase supplies of food for an institution, such as a college, a monastery or, as here, one of the Inns of Court (*temple* [567]). The Inns of Court are organizations of barristers which also act as law schools. Chaucer tells us that The Manciple is crafty enough to cheat his employers who are themselves clever enough to run any estate in England. He does not say what he does with the money he embezzles. In general we learn remarkably little about The Manciple, which may itself be significant.

567 Is Chaucer being ironic when he describes The Manciple as *gentil* (noble)?
570 **by taille** on credit, from the tally-stick, on which such transactions were recorded. The stick was split so that both creditor and debtor had an identical record.
571 **Algate** always.
   wayted watched, took care.
   achaat buying.
572 **ay biforn** always ahead (i.e. in profit).
573 In what way would it be God's grace that an uneducated person could trick many learned people?
574 **lewed** uneducated.
   pace surpass.
577 **curious** skilful.
581 **propre good** own wealth.
582 **but if** unless.
   wood mad.
583 Or live as economically as he wished.
586 **sette hir aller cappe** deceived them all. How does Chaucer's long account of the abilities of his victims affect our attitude to The Manciple's deceptions?

The Reeve

Normally a reeve was responsible for the practical part of estate management, checking on the condition of the lord's land and animals, and supervising the labour of his tenants. Chaucer's Reeve has also acquired some of the duties of the bailiff, supervising the stores (593), calculating the likely yield of the harvest (595), and presenting the accounts (600). We are told that he performs these duties well. Is he also corrupt, or does he merely oppress his fellow servants? Why are they so frightened of him (605)? How has he become able to lend money to his master (611)? The Reeve's thinness and his craftiness fit in with the humour (see Notes p. 51, line 333) of a choleric (*colerik*) man (587) but he lacks the equally characteristic emotional instability. Do you find any evidence of the choleric person's bad temper? Compare Chaucer's treatment of The Reeve with his attitude to The Manciple.

590 **top** top of his head.
  dokked cut short. Why does Chaucer give so much emphasis to his short hair?
592 **Ylyk a staf** like a staff.
593 **gerner** granary.
  bynne grain bin.
594 **on him wynne** get the better of him.
596 **yeldynge** yield.
597 **neet** cattle.
  dayerye dairy cattle.
598 **swyn** pigs.
  stoor livestock.
602 No one could prove that he owed anything.
603 **nas** (= *ne was*) was not.
  baillif farm manager, usually a reeve's superior but here responsible to him.
  hierde herdsman.
  hyne servant.
604 **sleighte** tricks.
  covyne deceit.
606 Why does The Reeve live away from other people?
609 **riche** richly.
  astored provided.
610 **subtilly** cunningly. The Reeve lends the lord his own money (*good* [611]), which he has embezzled.
612 The coat and hood will be The Reeve's reward.
613 Why does Chaucer say that The Reeve once learned a good trade (*myster*)?
616 **pomely** dappled.
  highte was called. Scot was a common name for a horse (*stot* [615]), especially in Norfolk.
618 Why is his knife rusty?
620 Bawdeswell (*Baldeswelle*) is in Norfolk, about fifteen miles north-west of Norwich. Some scholars have been encouraged to look for a real-life model for The Reeve by the fact that Chaucer

was once slightly involved in a court case about the manor of Bawdeswell.

621 **Tukked**   (his coat was) hitched up.

622 **route**   company. Does he ride at the back to avoid his enemy The Miller or because the rear is the best place from which to observe the other pilgrims? Does it matter that Chaucer here (and elsewhere) describes the pilgrims' behaviour on the journey which they have not yet begun?

The Summoner

In fourteenth-century England, ecclesiastical courts existed alongside the civil courts. Ecclesiastical courts, which were often presided over by the archdeacon (655), tried churchmen for all offences except treason, and tried lay people for offences against the Church such as non-payment of tithes, heresy and adultery. The civil courts tried lay people for all other offences against person, property and the state. Summoners were lay officials employed by the Church courts to deliver summonses to attend court and sometimes to provide information about wrongdoers. Many lay people resented the Church courts, and summoners were often satirized. They were accused of lechery because of their involvement in cases of adultery.

Chaucer describes The Summoner's corrupt practices, and attacks his drunkenness and his ignorance. But the portrait is overshadowed by The Summoner's facial disfigurement. Does Chaucer's description make you feel sympathetic or disgusted? What do you think of his explanation for the disease? Are we meant to draw a parallel between The Summoner's appearance and his moral state? Unusually, Chaucer dissociates himself from this pilgrim's opinions (659). Why? What should we think of The Summoner's 'good fellowship' and the mercy he shows to some sinners? What is the effect of his garland and his bread shield (666–8)?

624 **cherubynnes**   cherub's. Cherubim are angels of the second rank. Usually they are depicted as blue (seraphim are red) but some medieval authors confused the orders of angels. The angels' redness was thought to be caused by the flames of divine love. What causes The Summoner's red face? Is Chaucer being

ironic when he compares him to an angel? Perhaps the (slight) similarity between the roles makes the comparison funnier?

625 **saucefleem** covered with pimples. In *Chaucer and the Medieval Sciences* W. C. Curry argues that the pimples, the narrow (*narwe*) eyes and the loss of hair (627) indicate that The Summoner suffers from alopecia, a form of leprosy. Other scholars have made different diagnoses (scabies or syphilis).

626 From early Greek literature onwards the sparrow (*sparwe*) has been said to be lecherous.

627 **scalled** scabby (scall is a skin disease).
piled hairless.

629–30 Mercury (*quyk-silver*), lead monoxide (*lytarge*), sulphur (*brymstoon*), borax (*Boras*), white lead (*ceruce*) and cream of tartar (*oille of tartre*) are all possible treatments for skin diseases. Chaucer here uses technical language not, as he usually does, to show the pilgrim's knowledge but rather to emphasize the seriousness of the disease. (See Approaches p. 85.)

631 **byte** burn, scour.

632 **whelkes** pimples.

634–5 Medieval people thought that garlic, leeks and red wine would heat the blood and thus worsen diseases like The Summoner's. (Compare with line 626.)

636 **wood** mad.

638 It was proverbial that some people spoke Latin when drunk. Presumably most of them knew more phrases than The Summoner.

640 **decree** decretal, a legally binding statement by a pope, hence a law of the Church.

642 Many medieval texts mention jays being taught to imitate human speech. Equally the continual noise of the jay is often called 'chatter'.

643 **clepen** say.
'Watte' a shortened form of Walter. Perhaps Chaucer thinks of *Watte* as the sound a jay makes. Or perhaps *pope* together with *jay* (642) alludes to 'popinjay' (sometimes 'papejay') a parrot, who could be taught to imitate speech.

644 **grope** test, question.

645 **philosophie** learning.

646 **'Questio quid iuris'** is Latin for 'the question is which part of the law?' A lawyer might use this phrase in court, but The

Summoner says it because it is an all-purpose remark.

647 **harlot**   rascal. In what sense does Chaucer call him *gentil* and *kynde*?

649 **suffre**   allow (i.e. he would ignore the offence).
   for   in return for.

651 **atte fulle**   completely.

652 Some scholars explain this expression as 'trick someone', others as 'seduce a woman'.

654 **awe**   fear. The Summoner assures the sinner that if he pays up he need have no fear of being reported to the ecclesiastical court, or of the penalties there. There may be an implication (658) that even if the case comes to court the archdeacon can be bribed. (See Approaches pp. 102–6.)

655 **curs**   excommunication (compare 486).

659 Might this be a line in which we hear Chaucer speaking as author rather than as pilgrim?

660–1 'Every guilty man should fear excommunication because that will damn (literally, kill) as surely as absolution will save.' (See Notes to The Pardoner p. 70.)

662 **war hym**   let him beware.
   Significavit   writ of imprisonment (so called from the opening word of the document, which would be in Latin for the Church courts).

663 **In daunger**   in (his) control.
   at his owene gise   as he pleased.

664 **girles**   can refer to young people of both sexes.

665 **conseil**   secrets.
   al hir reed   advisor to all of them.

668 **cake**   loaf of bread. Does Chaucer mean to suggest that The Summoner is a glutton, or a fool, or is it a (possibly endearing) eccentricity to carry a loaf instead of a shield?

The Pardoner

Pardoners were employees of the Church, often priests, who sold pardons (or indulgences). In the medieval view, every sinful act had two aspects, an eternal aspect which involved turning away from God, and a temporal aspect which involved turning towards the world. If a sinner confessed his or her sins fully and showed contrition, a priest would give absolution, which is forgiveness for the eternal part of the sin, and a penance, which would compensate for the temporal part. A penance would usually be an act of charity or of devotion (such as saying a set number of prayers or visiting a particular shrine). It was possible to obtain, from the Pope or from a bishop, an indulgence to remove some or all of one's temporal guilt. An indulgence might be granted for exceptional help to the Church or in return for money.

The sale of indulgences became a way of converting guilt into income for the Church. The system was often abused and was much criticized. Indeed the abuse of indulgences was one of the factors which precipitated the Reformation of the Sixteenth century, when the Church was split. One of the actions of the Council of Trent (1545–63) which reformed the Catholic church was to end the sale of indulgences.

Chaucer follows William Langland in *Piers Plowman* (see Appendix p. 151–52) and other social satirists in making his Pardoner exploit his occupation for personal financial gain. Beyond that The Pardoner makes money by charging people for seeing or touching false relics which he carries around (694–704). Chaucer implies that his man is such an excellent pardoner (693) *because* he tricks people so outrageously and makes so much money. On the other hand he praised the quality of The Pardoner's participation in church services. Compare Chaucer's attitude to his Pardoner with Langland's.

Much critical attention has been devoted to The Pardoner's appearance and his sexual inclination. W. C. Curry in *Chaucer and the Medieval Sciences* argued that The Pardoner was a eunuch and that he and The Summoner were homosexual partners. The main evidence in favour of this view is: the thinness and length of The Pardoner's hair (675–9), his high pitched voice (688), his lack of a beard (689), Chaucer's belief that he was *a geldyng or a mare* (691), a possible pun involving their singing (673), the song sung (672) and the supposed medieval belief that the hare is a hermaphrodite (684). The interpretation of much of this evidence is disputed. The main alternative view is that The Pardoner was an effeminate heterosexual like the character Absolon in *The Miller's Tale*. In support of this one might cite The Pardoner's claim in his own prologue that he has a woman in every town. It has also been pointed out that The Pardoner must at most only have appeared to be a eunuch because a real eunuch could not be a priest (708–12). According to D. R. Howard in *Chaucer, His Life, His Works, His World* there is no evidence that the word *mare* (691) could mean 'male homosexual'. Some critics' attempts to connect The Pardoner's appearance with his sexual orientation probably involve stereotyping and an unconscious hostility to homosexuals.

669 Why does Chaucer call The Pardoner *gentil*?

670 The Hospital of St Mary of Rouncesval (Chaucer's *Rouncivale*) at Charing Cross, an Augustinian friary, was very active in the sale of indulgences and was involved in scandals over unauthorized sales in the 1380s. Chaucer's audience would probably have picked up the association of dishonesty.
compeer comrade.

671 Who had come directly from the papal court.

672 Probably a refrain from a popular song.

673 **stif burdoun** strong bass accompaniment (some critics find a phallic pun).

675 In physiognomy (see Notes to line 552, p. 64) yellow hair was said to indicate wild and unruly behaviour, thin hair guile and covetousness.

676 **strike** hank.
flex flax.

677 **ounces** small strands.

679 **colpons** strands.

681 **trussed** packed.
walet travel bag.

682 **Hym thoughte** it seemed to him.
jet fashion.

683 **Dischevelee** with hair unbound.
bare bare headed.

684 **glarynge eyen** bulging eyes.

685 **vernycle** a badge from the pilgrimage to Rome. The badge depicts St Veronica's handkerchief (kept in St Peter's) which is believed to carry an imprint of Christ's face.

687 **Bretful** brimful. Is there an ironic or mercenary implication in saying that the pardons were hot from Rome?

688 **smal** high-pitched.

691 How do you interpret this line?

692 **craft** trade. Berwick-on-Tweed is on the border with Scotland. Ware is just north of London. So presumably Chaucer means 'across the whole country'. (But there might perhaps be an anti-northern joke. Chaucer's associations were with Kent.)

694 **male** bag.

pilwe-beer pillowcase. Most medieval people venerated relics associated with Christ and the saints, but satirists often claimed that they were false, as most of them must have been.

695 **Oure Lady** the virgin Mary, mother of Christ.

696 **gobet** piece.

698 **hente** took (in the sense of 'called him').

699 **latoun** latten, brass.

702 **person** parson.

upon lond in the country. Is Chaucer making a comment here by reminding us of his Parson and suggesting a comparison?

703 **gat hym** obtained.

706 **apes** fools, dupes.

707 **atte laste** finally. What is the effect of *trewely*?

708 Does The Pardoner's reading, singing and preaching really make him a *noble ecclesiaste* in church? Might his high goat-like voice (688) suggest that there is some irony here?

710 The priest sings the offertory while the congregation give money. (Compare with 450–2.) Why does The Pardoner sing this part of the service best of all?

712 What does the phrase about smoothing (*affile*) his tongue to *wynne silver* (713) make us think of The Pardoner?

Explanation and Apology: Lines 715–46

At the end of the portraits Chaucer reminds us that he has told us all about the pilgrims and why they have come to Southwark, and he sets out the rest of his plan. First, he will narrate what happened on the evening that the company met, and then he will describe the pilgrimage itself. But before beginning he makes an elaborate apology. It will not be his fault if the language, stories and behaviour of the pilgrims are not always polite. His duty is to describe what happened. It is possible to read this section (725–42) almost as a statement of Chaucer's poetic creed: absolute fidelity to what was said, or, given the fictional status of the whole pilgrimage, absolute appropriateness (hence *proprely* [729]) to character (or narrative?). But the paragraph can also be read as an attempt to evade responsibility for what he has created: do not blame me for the bad taste and bad language which follows, I am only reporting what was said.

Chaucer also wants to apologize for not having sufficient intelligence always to place the pilgrims in their correct social position. Does he make this apology to warn his readers, to entice them, or to obtain their goodwill? Why does he take so long over it? And why is he prepared to own up to lack of wit (746) but anxious to escape the charge of *vileynye* (726, 740)?

715 **in a clause**   briefly.
718 Has the word *gentil* lost all sense of social superiority when it is applied to the Tabard?
719 **faste**   close. There were many inns in Southwark called *The Bell*.
721 **baren us**   conducted ourselves.
    ilke   same.
726 **n'arette it nat**   do not impute it to.
    vileynye   rudeness, lack of courtesy, boorishness. *Vileynye* is the behaviour suited to a villain, or common person. It is the opposite of *gentillesse*.
731 **after a man**   as someone else told it.
732 **moot reherce**   must repeat. Is it true that a narrator must repeat a story as exactly as possible? Why might Chaucer want to make this claim?
733 **if it be in his charge**   if it is entrusted to him.
734 However crudely (*rudeliche*) and freely (*large*) he may speak.
736 Is there something humorous in the tone here, as Chaucer explains that it would be wrong to make things up (*feyne*)?
738 'He must repeat one word as much as another' (i.e. the crude words must be included just as much as the innocent ones).
739 I cannot think of anything Christ says in the *Bible* which offers a precedent for the *vileynye* of some of Chaucer's language.
741 **kan hym rede**   knows how to read him. Chaucer cites this remark of Plato from Boethius's (c480–524) *The Consolation of Philosophy*, which he had translated from Latin, rather than from Plato's own works (in Greek) only two of which were known in Western Europe in the Fourteenth century.

742 **cosyn** closely related.

744 **Al** although, if. Do you think Chaucer is apologizing for the order of the portraits or for the action which will follow? Is he telling us that it has now become difficult to observe the niceties of social order with exactness, or that he does not wish to do so? This might reflect a more general social anxiety, as if Chaucer recognized that in his lifetime the social status of some groups was changing and feared that this might lead him to make mistakes and become involved in quarrels.

746 Chaucer insists on his own foolishness in many of his works. Sometimes he is straightforwardly ironic, sometimes conventionally modest, and sometimes deviously denying responsibility for what he has written. Which is it here?

The Host and his Proposal: Lines 747–821

Modern critical fashion is generally against attempting to discover real-life originals for the pilgrims, but most people agree that the real innkeeper Harry Baily (so named in *The Cook's Prologue*) was Chaucer's model. (See Approaches p. 107.) Harry Baily had acted as member of parliament for Southwark, tax-collector and coroner. There is a record of his carrying money from the Custom House to the Treasury at a time when Chaucer was Controller of Customs.

In the *General Prologue* The Host is open, merry and practical. He makes a proposal which will assure the pilgrims of an enjoyable journey and his inn of another grand feast on their return. The Host's speech is very carefully constructed in order to persuade the pilgrims to agree to his plan. First, he praises the assembled company, suggesting that he wants to repay them for their happiness with a plan that will increase their enjoyment. He is careful to emphasize that it will cost them nothing (761–8). This opening is intended to establish a climate of goodwill between himself and the pilgrims. Next he reminds the pilgrims of their purpose: to visit the shrine of St Thomas and to enjoy themselves on the journey (769–72) and argues that dumb silence will not contribute to their aim. Therefore they should band together under his leadership and he will guarantee them an enjoyable time (775–82). Why does he seek their agreement in principle before going into the details of his plan?

Once they have agreed he outlines his scheme (788–801) and he concludes by reminding them that they will enjoy themselves, by insisting that he will pay his own expenses, and by warning them that whoever contests his judgement will have to pay for what they all drink on the journey (802–09). What sort of an image of himself does The Host project in this speech? What do we learn about him? Who has the most to gain from the arrangement?

The Host's plan calls for two tales from each pilgrim on the way to Canterbury and two more each on the way back. This would have resulted in a collection of at least 120 tales (allowing that Chaucer miscounts and that at least one person joins the pilgrimage *en route*). In its incomplete state *The Canterbury Tales* contains twenty-four tales (four of them incomplete). In *The Parson's Prologue* The Host announces that only one more tale is required to complete the project and the journey to Canterbury (implying a one way journey and one tale each). The introductory passages to the individual tales suggest that Chaucer changed his mind about the overall plan more than once between the statement of the plan in the *General Prologue* (probably composed in the late 1380s) and his death in 1400.

747 **Greet chiere**   warm welcome.
750 **wel to drynke us leste**   we were very pleased to drink.
751 **semely**   suitable.
752 **marchal**   master of ceremonies.
753 **eyen stepe**   bright (or large) eyes.
754 **Chepe**   Cheapside, one of the main streets of medieval London.
756 What is the point of saying that The Host lacked nothing in manliness (*manhod*)? (Compare with line 167.)
760 'When we had paid our bills' (the night before leaving). Perhaps there is some implication that The Host wants to assure himself that the company really is sufficiently wealthy before explaining his idea. He is practical as well as welcoming.
763 **by my trouthe**   by my faith.
766 **Fayn**   gladly.
    doon yow myrthe   make you merry.
767 **I am... bythoght**   I have thought of.
768 Why does The Host say that his plan will cost them nothing?
769 **God yow speede**   may God give you success.

770 May the heavenly martyr give you your reward!
772 **shapen yow** intend.
    talen tell stories.
778 To abide by my decision.
779 **werken** do.
782 If you don't enjoy yourselves you may strike off my head!
784 **conseil** decision.
785 **make it wys** raise difficulties. Is Chaucer suggesting that there was anything wrong with the way they agreed?
786 **graunted hym** agreed to his proposal.
787 **voirdit** verdict.
    as hym leste as it pleased him.
789 But do not be indignant, I ask you.
791 **to shorte with** in order to shorten.
798 The most instructive and enjoyable tales.
799 **oure aller cost** all of our expense.
804 **Right... cost** entirely at my own expense.
805 **withseye** contest.
807 **vouche sauf** agree.
809 **shape me** prepare myself.
814 **reportour** record keeper.
816 **at his devys** according to his wishes.
817 **In heigh and lough** in all matters.
819 The wine was fetched (*fet*) in order to seal the agreement.

The Pilgrims Set Out: Lines 822–58

In the morning Harry Baily asserts the authority which the pilgrims have agreed to give him. He reminds them of the penalty for disobeying his command and announces the beginning of the competition. Rather than choose the first storyteller himself, he organizes a lottery. By chance, destiny, or the manoeuvrings of The Host, The Knight draws the short straw and is chosen to tell the first story. What do we learn about The Host and The Knight from their exchange? What do we learn about the other pilgrims from their reaction?

823 **aller cok** rooster for us all.
824 What is the implication of calling the pilgrims a flock?

825 **a litel... paas**   just above walking speed.

826 **the Wateryng of Seint Thomas**   a stream where the horses could drink, two miles along the road to Canterbury.

830 If you will stand by last night's words.

835 **ferrer twynne**   go further.

840 **lat be**   leave off.
   shamefastnesse   modesty.

841 **studieth**   deliberate, brood (with a pun for The Clerk).

844 **aventure... sort... cas**   Does the use of three such closely related words (roughly: chance, luck or destiny) indicate that The Host fixed the draw so that The Knight would start? Is there other evidence?

847 **resoun**   reasonable.

849 **what... mo**?   what more is there to say?

851 Why does Chaucer emphasize The Knight's modest acceptance? Is he making a statement about the society formed by the pilgrims? Was The Knight reluctant to begin? Is it an example of his politeness?

Approaches

Approaches through Chaucer's Life and Times

Background to the Poem

Many people in the Twentieth century have held the view that English Literature started with the works of Geoffrey Chaucer, in the second half of the Fourteenth century (he probably started writing the *General Prologue* in 1388). There was work produced much earlier than this, however: manuscripts of poetry even survive from dates earlier than the year 1000. By the time Chaucer began *The Canterbury Tales* more manuscripts were surviving and, whereas during the earlier Middle Ages a variety of dialects had been used, the language for literature was becoming standardized through the use of the London English which he employed.

The *General Prologue* is the first part of a large poem, the final work in Chaucer's career. He was in his mid-forties when he began the poem. It is in fact a kind of introduction to *The Canterbury Tales*, which is altogether a larger although unfinished work. The device that Chaucer affords himself is the opportunity to describe, in a varied, but sometimes critical and often humorous manner, a cross section of types of people drawn from different walks of life in medieval society. He proves to be an expert in understanding the natures of these people assembled in the Tabard in Southwark. After the descriptions the story-telling challenge is offered by The Host, a man by the name of Harry Baily. Having provided the best possible welcome for this *so myrie a compaignye* (764), especially in terms of food and drink, The Host suggests that, in order to make the journey more enjoyable, they are to tell their stories and he will judge which is the best. All the pilgrims will then stand supper for the winner of the story-telling competition.

It should not come as a great surprise that Chaucer should have wanted to write a poem based on the telling of stories. He had written a number of earlier poems, including dream-poems in which he, the narrator, was the dreamer; in *Troilus and Criseyde* he appeared, rather like a novelist of later centuries, to be reading the story rather than telling it; and in *The Legend of Good Women* which he in fact abandoned as his last poem before starting on *The Canterbury Tales*, he saw The God of Love as an apparition who forced him to compile a variety of stories about women who had died as martyrs to the cause of love. In each of these cases he, Chaucer – the person, the scholar and the poet – was able to take part in the poem whilst at the same time he could stand back from what was happening.

A similar narrative technique occurs in the *General Prologue*. Here Chaucer is part of the assembled company of pilgrims but by comparison with the characters he so richly and vividly describes, he – and remember that he too is a pilgrim – rather merges into the background and appears to report most faithfully and objectively what he observes, often without judging traits in character. This 'standing back', in the role of 'spectator-commentator' gives him a lot of flexibility. On the one hand he can appear to be describing his fellow pilgrims in meticulous, factual detail, when in fact he might be ironically pointing out their shortcomings or eccentricities, and on the other hand he has the capacity to intervene with his own voice on occasions, often in a rather understated and retiring manner. Having, for example, described The Cook by emphasizing his culinary skill, Chaucer invites us to consider a possible contradiction in the man's worth by giving his opinion that it is a shame about the poisonous ulcer on his leg:

> But greet harm was it, as it thoughte me,
> That on his shyne a mormal hadde he. (385–6)

Following his admiration of the character's professional skill, Chaucer has suddenly, if rather unassertively, put the man in his place by voicing his own opinion that it is a shame he has an ulcer. A lively sense of The Cook at work has been created only to be undermined by Chaucer's personal intervention with a telling comment at a moment in the poem which he carefully chooses. An association between the ulcer and the food is suggested to the mind of the reader through the juxtaposition of the lines describing the *blankmanger* (387) and the *mormal* (386).

However, it is not too often that Chaucer himself becomes directly involved in passing comment on his fellow pilgrims. If anything, whilst he remains discreetly in the background, it is Harry Baily, The Host, who makes his presence felt with his enthusiastic idea at the end, for the competition. (See the suggestion in the Notes pp. 74–5 as to why The Host may be so keen to entertain the pilgrims again on their return.)

What do you think of this tone of polite observation and discreet description? It could be that his comments are all the more striking when Chaucer passes judgement on his fellows. Would you find him more or less convincing as a judge of character if he were continually telling us his opinions?

Activity

One way of grouping the pilgrims is given to you in The Notes p. 31. Are there ways of grouping them according to how much Chaucer admires or dislikes them? Into which category would you place The Knight, (p. 2), The Prioress (p. 4), The Monk, (p. 6), The Franklin (p. 10), The Ploughman (p. 16), The Summoner (p. 19)?

Discussion

Some of the categories you may have thought of are: those characters he openly admires; those whom he mocks and criticizes but still likes; those whom he idealizes – makes perfect or larger than life; those whose behaviour or morality irritates or disgusts him.

Another question that occurs to me is whether there is any change in tone when Chaucer becomes more critical.

Whilst describing the other pilgrims, Chaucer, for the most part, gives the impression that he remains detached as an observer, and succeeds in conveying what appears to be a straightforward account of his characters. These accounts, or portraits, are frequently made up of physical, professional and biographical details. At a superficial glance this selection of traits can give the impression that he is merely standing back from the society whose representatives he has assembled around him and that he is making no moral judgement about that society. How likely do you think this is?

I find that the description of The Merchant (p. 9) offers another example of Chaucer choosing his moment to make a subtle personal comment in addition to writing simply what he has observed (or apparently doing this!). In this portrait he presents a life-like picture of a man with a carefully-tended forked beard, elegantly and neatly dressed, wearing an expensive fur hat and fastidiously clasped boots, sitting high in the saddle of his horse. Then there is an impression of his preoccupations in speech and a commentary on his management of money and profit. These traits bring The Merchant to life as a man full of his own importance. Look again at the physical description. Can you see his haughty and rather distant character being created through the physical details even before mention of anything else?

With what appears to be effective timing Chaucer waits until the end of the portrait before making a comment of his own. By this time the physical description and account of The Merchant's behaviour have prepared us for a view that he may be a fraud. This reaches quite a climax:

> So estatly was he of his governaunce
> With his bargaynes and with his chevyssaunce,
> For sothe he was a worthy man with alle...   (281–3)

But then Chaucer cuts the portrait short by surprising us with the news that he cannot even remember the man's name! Do you think this is significant? There is no reason why he should have known his name but why does he bother to emphasize the fact? After all, he does not choose to do so with the other pilgrims, who remain unnamed.

Is this a strong or mild intervention? Why does Chaucer make a direct intervention only very rarely? Is it possible that he is not really intending to judge his characters? Or are moral judgements made in other ways?

Sources

Such a capacity for the narrator's voice to move in and out of his poem becomes even more important when the tales themselves begin. Another feature developed from his earlier works is the variety of styles he is able to call upon. As the poem progresses beyond the descriptions in the *General Prologue*, and the tales themselves are told, he demonstrates considerable versatility in his use of a huge variety of styles, drawing on a great many literary traditions, some of which reflect the character of each pilgrim as it has been described in the *General Prologue*.

As you know from the Notes (p. 39), Chaucer was clearly influenced by the French courtly poem, the *Roman de la Rose*. You can compare the two poems by looking at the opening to the French poem. (See Appendix pp. 150.) He also drew on an idea from the Medieval Estates Satire in which characters represent their class, calling or profession and are shown, satirically, to fall short of what might have been expected of them. They were mocked, the fun usually had by showing faults associated with their trade, class or occupation. In describing a hypocritical friar, a thieving miller, a bankrupt merchant, and others, Chaucer was following this tradition from the Estates Satire.

This model of Estates Satire has come to be seen as more important recently. There was an assumption that the *General Prologue* was an original idea but Jill Mann, in particular, has questioned this in her book, *Chaucer and Medieval Estates Satire*. 'Estate' here means something along the lines of 'station', 'class' or 'status'. In medieval life people ought to have been content with their own status and their behaviour needed to be kept in line with what would have been expected of them. This expectation would have been divinely ordained (decreed by God) and the good of society was dependent on everybody observing the rules of their status. Jill Mann said:

> I shall be claiming that the *Prologue* is an example of a neglected Medieval genre – that both its form and its content proclaim it to be part of the literature dealing with the 'estates' of society. (p. 1.)

Thus, even though there are lots of original lines and ideas in the poem, its origins may not have been at all new.

Chaucer's Society

Chaucer's knowledge of society was immense and varied. A close reading of the poem draws attention to the versatility of the work. He switches from an account of the crusades to life in the farmyard, from sea to land, from Church to trade: offering a revealing and often very humorous view of his contemporary society.

Geoffrey Chaucer's own varied life suggests why he might have possessed such a detailed knowledge of fourteenth century society. (See Chronology on pp. 122–3 for an outline of Chaucer's life.)

As a wholesale wine merchant his father was a mercantile man but the family was also a very important one, connected to the Royal Household. In 1357 he joined the household of the Earl and Countess of Ulster. (You will realize how important his position was because the Earl of Ulster was in fact Prince Lionel, third son of Edward III.) He fought in the French campaign of 1359–60, during which he was captured and ransomed. He later worked as an attendant in the court of Edward III and was Controller of Customs in the Port of London from 1374 until 1386. Although never a professional poet as such, he showed considerable interest in the works of Italian writers such as Dante, Petrarch and Boccaccio which he was introduced to on his visits to Italy on royal business in the 1370s. Thus, his background had brought him into contact with royalty, courtiers, the military, merchants and tradesmen, innkeepers and travellers. His varied professional and courtly background allowed him to experience a whole host of different types of people.

His period was a changing world, although it was still basically a feudal society. (You can read about this in the discussion of The Knight in the Notes [pp. 31–2].)

In spite of the Black Death – a plague which by 1350 had reduced England's population by about a third – the second half of the Fourteenth century was a relatively prosperous time in the Middle Ages. A reduced labour market (i.e. by the plagues) had made many peasants better off, although on the other hand, many great landowners, including the Church, struggling to maintain and acquire accustomed wealth, resorted to oppressive and extortionate measures against their often poor and humble tenants (notice the fear that The Reeve, who managed his lord's estate, inspires in those he deals with on the land [605]).

One thing that seems very important is that Chaucer may actually have witnessed some of the gruesome events of the Peasants' Revolt. Living as he did in Aldgate at the time it is quite likely that he saw the arrival of the mob, the burning down of John of Gaunt's palace and the various beheadings of local dignitaries, including the Archbishop of Canterbury. It is said that a lot of bodies were left piled high by the side of the river, near Chaucer's home.

Industry was also changing, beginning to centre on growing urban areas, often near ports, partly to meet the new demands of an export trade for wool, but also because of the use of fulling-mills ('fulling' removed grease from the wool) which saw the clothing industry begin to flourish in towns and villages near rivers.

Chaucer's Expertize

We get only a glimpse of his understanding of this developing world in the *General Prologue* – he shows more of it in the tales. What he displays is frequently a sort of specialist knowledge which reveals his classical learnedness, a seasoned wisdom in the ways of the world and also a technical understanding of such subjects as science, astrology, medicine, navigation and business.

In a typically modest tone he hints that a full understanding of the Pilgrims is within his capabilities when he says, near the beginning:

> But nathelees, whil I have tyme and space,
> Er that I ferther in this tale pace,
> Me thynketh it acordaunt to resoun
> To telle yow al the condicioun
> Of ech of hem, so as it semed me,
> And whiche they weren, and of what degree,
> And eek in what array that they were inne. (35–41)

He also had a wide knowledge of the work that his characters would have been doing. The Sergeant of the Law (p. 10) is mocked because of his pompous nature, but this touch of individuality blends with the plausible portrait of the man as a representative of the legal profession. Chaucer clearly knows all about what lawyers did: this man has been a judge at the court of assizes, having been given a royal commission to preside there with full judicial powers. He is also a successful buyer of land; he has an extensive knowledge of all the legal cases drawn up since the days of King William, is expert himself at drawing up legal documents and knows all the statutes by rote. At the end of this description Chaucer turns to the portrait of the Franklin (p. 10) and shows just as much knowledge about his work – particularly his 'housekeeping' skills.

Worldly knowledge is not confined to what is morally acceptable: Chaucer seems to know only too well of the questionable practices of The Miller (p. 17) and The Shipman (p. 12), and the wiliness of The Manciple (p. 17). He is just as much in touch with what is criminal and illicit as he is with the world of business and science.

Chaucer is sometimes inclined to present his knowledge in catalogues of detail. His great love of lists of things perhaps reveals a desire to show off his own encyclopaedic knowledge of an expanding world. Mindful of his standing with the other pilgrims, this 'encyclopaedism', as the lists have been called, may also be an attempt to impress the reader with authoritative examples called upon to reinforce the points he is making.

These lists can lend a realism to the descriptions of characters through use of everyday objects, as is the case with The Prioress, who fed her small dogs: *With rosted flessh, or milk and wastel-breed.* (147).

The Knight's coat of mail (76), the *takel* (106), of The Yeoman, the rural stock that The Reeve looks after (597–8) all help to convince us of the real nature of their work and behaviour.

In other, perhaps grander moments, he uses this approach to exaggerate the distinctiveness and authority of characters who can be seen as the finest of their types, lending them a superiority. How does this happen with The Knight (p. 2), The Doctor of Physic (p. 13), and The Reeve (p. 18)?

The effect can also be to mock the characters, using his lists in an emphatically satirical mode. The Wife of Bath's impressive background of attendance on pilgrimages is listed in the same style as The Knight's on crusades:

> At Rome she hadde been, and at Boloigne,
> In Galice at Seint-Jame, and at Coloigne.   (465–6)

But we soon learn that this devotion may have been for dubious reasons. The Summoner's scabrous skin complaints cannot be cured by any substances available in medicine:

> Ther nas quyk-silver, lytarge, ne brymstoon,
> Boras, ceruce, ne oille of tartre noon...   (629–30)

Is there anything that could cure his disreputable nature?

Activity

Choose one or more of these areas of Chaucer's general knowledge and show what he knew of the subject: astronomy and medicine (e.g. The Doctor of Physic p. 13); cookery (e.g. The Cook p. 12, The Franklin p. 10); geography (e.g. The Merchant p. 9, The Shipman p. 12); working on the land (e.g. The Yeoman p. 4, The Ploughman p. 16, The Reeve p. 18). On which other subjects did he have a strong general knowledge?

Discussion

Once we have come to realize just how much Geoffrey Chaucer did seem to know about the world around him we often want to say that the poem is a sort of documentary of medieval society. But be careful with this interpretation!

Because he was writing within the traditions available to him in medieval poetry it is important for us, in the Twentieth century, not to over-exaggerate the significance of the 'documentary' interpretation of the poem at the expense of recognizing it as part of a literary tradition. In the course of *The Canterbury Tales* as a whole he draws on a huge variety of story-telling forms: the courtly romance, the moral exemplar, parody, mock-heroic beast fable, bawdy fabliau. But for the *General Prologue* there were perhaps three features of most significance.

First, he undoubtedly drew on the style and arrangement of French courtly literature – a style of writing which was very conventional, tending to idealize rather than represent the real world, often with a very static, polite, pure and formal tone.

Secondly, he used a developing realistic tradition of medieval literature in which he would have learnt to characterize his people in a more down-to-earth sort of way using domestic imagery in familiar settings, along with colloquial and even impolite descriptions.

Thirdly, he was also writing with an outlook which held that there was a connection between literature and morality. We at least know that he was aware of this from the lines near the end of *The Nun's Priest's Tale*:

> But ye that holden this tale a folye,
> As of a fox, or of a cok and hen,
> Taketh the moralite, good men.
>> (Riverside Fragment VII 3438–40)

(The Nun's Priest is one of the characters who accompanies The Prioress. He is not given a portrait in the *General Prologue*.)

Approaches through Chaucer's Subject Matter

The Messages in the Opening Lines

Before introducing the pilgrims, Chaucer begins the *General Prologue* with forty-two opening lines which set a tone for some of the meanings in the poem as a whole. A world undergoing its rebirth in spring is celebrated. It is an uplifting and enthusiastic start to a poem. Look at how the sheer sensuous energy is established through the personification of the months of March and April, the latter month having:

> ... bathed every veyne in swich licour
> Of which vertu engendred is the flour;   (3–4)

Then look at the vivid way that:

> ... Zephirus eek with his sweete breeth
> Inspired hath in every holt and heeth
> The tendre croppes ...   (5–7)

This traditional opening with its partly elevated style and its vision of universal change and rebirth is contrasted with the more realistic description of the preparation for pilgrimage, in the Tabard in South London. Having originally had our attention drawn towards the universally significant realms of seasonal, cosmic and natural existence (1–11) and then on the yearning for foreign pilgrimage engendered in such an inspiring new season (12–13), Chaucer soon brings the reader's focus right down to earth:

> Bifil that in that seson on a day,
> In Southwerk at the Tabard as I lay...   (19–20)

Do you notice a change in the style here? It seems curious that, following such an elevated opening, Chaucer should switch to a more chatty, anecdotal and familiar kind of language. It is worth pausing for thought on the possible connections between the sensuous opening and the purposes of a medieval pilgrimage. Certainly these two areas of experience might not, at a superficial glance, appear automatically related.

Many critics who have analysed the opening have suggested that there is indeed a connection between the energy of nature as it is here presented (the climax being the nightingale's nocturnal incitement of spirit) and the enthusiasm for indulgence of one sort or another which was beginning to characterize late medieval pilgrimages. The emphasis during the description of spring is most definitely on the creativity and energy of the season. It is not an emphasis on the reality of the season in England, although there are elements of natural life which seem very real indeed.

Activity

Read again the Notes on pp. 28–9 on the long opening sentence. What are the different elements in the sentence? It is important to think about the relationship between the opening and the rest of the *General Prologue*. Is there a contrast? What do you notice about the varieties of style used at the beginning?

Discussion

The vitality of the first eleven lines personifies the natural world in such a way that we can sense spring itself coming to life as if the sap is rising and the world reawakening before our very eyes. There is a lively breathlessness anyway in the length and unforced climax of the first sentence and the excitement is further established through the sensuous alliteration of *shoures soote* (1), *swich licour* (3) and *sweete breeth* (5). The ram, zodiacal sign of Aries, may have been a symbol of sexual potency and the nightingale supposedly sang continuously for fifteen days in the mating season. You will also see from the Note on line 11, (p. 30) the suggestion of a possible sexual connotation in the deliberately understated phrase (*So priketh hem nature in hir corages*).

Activity

Is the opening ironic? What has all this earthly voluptuousness to do with pilgrimages?

Discussion

Religious pilgrimages – journeys to sanctified places, originally in The Holy Land – began as early as the Second century. The aims of these journeys were the veneration and collection of relics, articles which were often stripped from the shrines of saints, and brought home. Original pilgrimages offered religious zealots an ideal opportunity for a quiet period of undisturbed contemplation and self-examination. Salvation, atonement, redemption and worship were all sought or practised. However, by the Middle Ages, as roads had improved and journeys had been made relatively easier, many pilgrimages came to be more like excursions. No longer were they attractive only to devout zealots whose sole purpose would have been spiritual, but they were increasingly joined by ordinary folk from all walks of life. Far from maintaining a mode of behaviour which was entirely in keeping with their contemplative purpose, the medieval pilgrimage saw the enthusiastic emergence of more worldly, social and indulgent traditions, story-telling amongst them. The behaviour on many pilgrimages was condemned as improper by the Church. Thus, the idea of the pilgrimage as a very serious and pious type of journey was ripe for mockery. Certainly Chaucer's wry comment in line 467 that The Wife of Bath *koude muchel of wandrynge by the weye*, when talking about her earlier holy journeys suggests that she at least has enjoyed her travels for reasons which might have been worldly rather than reverent.

Towards the end of the introductory remarks, Chaucer makes it quite clear that his assembled company are to be well looked after:

> The chambres and the stables weren wyde,
> And wel we weren esed atte beste.   (28–9)

He later reveals that they have been eating and drinking plentifully:

> Greete chiere made oure Hoost us everichon,
> And to the soper sette he us anon.
> He served us with vitaille at the beste;
> Strong was the wyn, and wel to drynke us leste.   (747–50)

Was it simply polite of Chaucer to record The Host's welcome or do you think he wants to make a point about how the pilgrims spent their night before pilgrimage?

What connections or contradictions can you detect between the various elements: between the potent description of the rebirth of the world in spring; the sexual undertones in some of the lines; the devout purpose of pilgrimage; and the apparently indulgent evening spent by Chaucer's pilgrims in the Tabard?

The Sondry Folk from Medieval Society

Just as the traditional drought of March has been impregnated by the refreshing showers of April and warmed by the west wind of classical mythology, so pilgrims are stirred to travel to the shrines which have helped to heal them when they have been sick. Once the poem has moved from its supernatural and natural levels and become particular and realistic – in the Tabard – there is an irony associated with the motives of pilgrimage. The pilgrims may be motivated to undertake a pilgrimage, but consider carefully what sorts of things motivate them normally, from what we learn in the descriptions of their lives.

Chaucer's cross-section from society is shown to be a group of energetic and active people. Most of them live their lives to the full, but not always for the good of others. Whilst some of them, such as The Knight and The Parson, behave only in a proper and praise-worthy manner, entirely within the expectations of their callings, others, such as The Summoner and The Pardoner are motivated entirely by the pursuit of avarice and a desire to cheat and swindle those with whom they come into contact. The Clerk and The Ploughman are the two other exceptions as their morals are also unquestionable, and the remainder fall in between the somewhat idealized Knight and Parson and the despicable Summoner and Pardoner. There are indeed all sorts of characters present in the inn, and this random, unforced nature of the grouping is something which Chaucer stresses by calling it *a compaignye / Of sondry folk, by aventure yfalle* (24–5).

It is a random group of people but that is not the same as saying that they are ordinary. Quite the opposite, many are described as the best of their type, or the most successful. The fullness of their lives and the fact that each of them individually is described as doing at least as much as, if not more, than their contemporaries, provides an ideal opportunity to study the full range of motives which lead to a variety of human actions. Thus greed, pride, lust and vanity influence the dispositions of so many of these characters and the insight offered by Chaucer in his version of fourteenth century society becomes applicable universally to people of all ages.

Activity

Try and find references which present the characters and their behaviour in an exaggerated and sometimes even incomparable manner. These will be the sorts of phrases which make them stand out as the most successful of their kind. In particular make a list of these exaggerated generalized points from the descriptions of The Knight (p. 2), The Friar (p. 7), The Shipman (p. 12) and The Wife of Bath (p. 14). Why has he so often chosen to make the pilgrims appear to be ideal individuals for his purposes?

Discussion

As he begins to *telle . . . the condicioun* (38) of this *felaweshipe* (32) of pilgrims he begins with the most important, The Knight (p. 2), whose perfect chivalry personifies ideals of medieval Christianity and military power. This man takes pride of place. Accompanying him is his son, the young Squire (p. 3), and one servant, a Yeoman (p. 4). If the description of The Knight sets a standard by which we can judge the morality of the other characters, the account of The Squire seems to take up again the vitality and energy of the opening with a perspective on his youthful manhood and sexual energy. Next, The Yeoman is a sturdy young man who takes pride in his calling and whom Chaucer seems to admire for his skills as a forester.

The following group of three ecclesiastical characters, The Prioress (p. 4), The Monk (p. 6), and The Friar (p. 7), display traits of worldliness in their characters but each is largely tolerated by Chaucer as they seem to appeal to him in some respects. The Prioress's appeal comes through her elegant femininity, The Monk's through his virile love of a good life and The Friar's his arrogant strength of personality and skilful accomplishments, in spite of his roguish behaviour.

This first cluster have been important members of society and there have been only mild ironic hints about any of their double standards and shortcomings. To some extent this respectful tone changes when Chaucer comes to the next group which is mostly drawn from a developing bourgeoisie in society – remember it was a society in which trade and money were becoming more important: only The

Clerk breaks the sequence of a group whose overriding motives in life are to make money or climb social ladders connected with the trappings of wealth. It may even have been a deliberate decision of Chaucer's to place his description of The Clerk (p. 9) in amongst this group to contrast his inability to make a living with the money-grabbing nature of The Merchant (p. 9), the pomposity of The Sergeant of the Law (p. 10), the indulgence of The Franklin (p. 10), the distinguished but self-important behaviour of The Guildsmen (p. 11) (and their rascal of a cook (p. 12)), the roguery of The Shipman (p. 12) and the prominent wealth of The Doctor of Physic (p. 13).

The highly individualistic portrayal of The Wife of Bath (p. 14) whose sexuality and racy past are celebrated along with her ostentatious appearance is contrasted with perhaps the most idealized versions of life in The Parson (p. 15) and his humble brother, The Ploughman (p. 16). Their unstinting goodness and charity give way to a group who, in The Miller (p. 17), The Manciple (p. 17) and The Reeve (p. 18), reveal characteristics of shrewd profit motive and calculated ambition. Finally Chaucer turns to the most scurrilous pair, The Summoner (p. 19) and The Pardoner (p. 20) for whom the irony appears now to be anything but mild or harmless. Whereas earlier he shows a tolerance and even a sneaking respect for the foibles and failings of his characters, he is, in the end, viciously satirical about this pair who are unashamedly devious and corrupt. Do you think he is condemning them?

The Friar and The Prioress are the only ones to have been given a name. The Shipman himself is not identified, but his boat is – *the Maudelayne* (410). But this does not mean that the company remain anonymous representatives of their type or class. Far from it, many of them are presented in such a personal and realistic way that they come fully to life as individuals.

Activity

What sorts of personal details are used to bring the characters to life? To help you think about this, study closely three pilgrims who are made to seem very realistic, e.g. The Monk (p. 6), The Merchant (p. 9) and The Miller (p. 17).

Discussion

The catalogue of The Knight's crusades, the background knowledge of The Squire's military apprenticeship, the ins and outs of financial and trade activities practised by the mercantile pilgrims, and not least, the impressive list of medical authorities known to The Doctor (p. 13), all document the work of prominent or typical members of medieval society.

But although the traditions of their trades are catalogued there are also moments of vivid personal detail which prevent the portraits from ever becoming dry, lifeless or barren. The poem is immensely flexible; there is a lot of movement between one mode of description and another. Chaucer switches unexpectedly from an account of the work or background of a character to a very revealing instance of personal appearance or personal habit. Often this combination of purposes is achieved almost at random, casually, unsystematically, as if there is recognition that human life cannot easily be classified or organized. It is as if the work, the appearance, the behaviour, the motivations, achievements and shortcomings of medieval people – perhaps all people of all ages – cannot be detached one from the other and, accordingly, Chaucer's hotchpotch of descriptive technique attempts to express the vitality of human life in a varied tapestry.

Have you noticed the range of individualizing characteristics used for the pilgrims through this Activity?

Another one who both represents a type and is also vividly portrayed, using a variety of techniques to bring him to life is The Friar. See how a combination of purposes works. As you get to know this rascal, you will find, as he goes about his work as a licenciat, numerous examples of the hypocrisy associated with many other men of his calling. These define his office. But then go through the portrait and see what you notice about the man personally, particularly between lines 233 and 239 and from line 259 onwards. What sort of man is this *Huberd* (269) and how does knowledge of his individual personality complement what you learn of him as a representative of the Franciscan Order?

The Age of Chivalry

In the Golden Age of Chivalry medieval knights exemplified the very ideals of chivalric behaviour and morals. The strength of the Order of Knighthood lay not so much in its numbers but in the acceptance of its ideas, and medieval people certainly believed in these ideals. In the Notes (p. 33) see the comment on lines 45–6 where Chaucer sets out the qualities in his *parfit gentil knyght*.

The note of perfection in The Knight's chivalrous character provides the poem with an honourable start. This is out of keeping with many of the characteristics of other pilgrims who are far from perfect. The Knight's honourable nature appears to set a standard so that, although we might find it difficult to believe that any single man could be so morally noble, we are able to use him as a yardstick by which to measure the greed and hyprocisy of many of the others. (However, see Notes pp. 31–4 for interpretations which question the 'true' nature of The Knight.)

Chivalry, in the late Middle Ages, suggested a religious, social and moral code as well as military 'prowess'. In his account of The Knight, Chaucer complements the idealistic abstractions of *chivalrie*, / *Trouthe… honour, fredom* and *curteisie*, (45–6) by a series of powerful adjectives and adverbs which stress The Knight's abundant goodness and give recognition to his idealized character:

> Ful worthy was he in his lordes werre,
> And therto hadde he riden, no man ferre,
> As wel in cristendom as in hethenesse...   (47–9)

Do you think the description makes him appear more as an idealized type – i.e. of knights in general – or as a real knight? Although the overall quality of his perfect character may be hard to believe, John M. Manly has suggested that he may have been based on a real knight who as a contemporary and acquaintance of Chaucer's, would have taken part in the series of crusades listed.

As well as establishing his worthiness through a description of his character, Chaucer notes his prowess with an impressive list of the battles he has fought in the crusades, stressing the practical application to which he has honourably and courageously put his Christian values. The only note of realism comes at the end of the portrait with a few details of his modest appearance and the information that he has joined the pilgrimage with no time to change his dress as he has so recently returned from a campaign abroad. As if to emphasize the chivalry of The Knight, Chaucer notes that his tunic was stained by the rust from his coat of mail. Do you think that these touches of realism may even add to the idealized portrait of The Knight? We do not have to think of realism and idealization as exclusive of each other.

To an extent the tone of ideal honour and chivalry is extended in the enthusiastic and vibrant account of The Knight's son, the young Squire. In the feudal system, squires were really young knights in the making, next in command. They had one servant with them, a Yeoman. If it is the youthfulness of the Squire which becomes emphasized through such a vivid, sensual and admiring portrait, what is it that gets emphasized in the account of The Yeoman?

Activity

Go through the first three descriptions, of The Knight (p. 2), The Squire (p. 3) and The Yeoman (p. 4),. What do you learn of their appearances? What do their actions and exploits tell us about the quality of their characters? Can you find evidence to suggest Chaucer's attitude to these characters?

Discussion

With the curious exceptions of The Clerk, The Parson and The Ploughman, Chaucer follows his descriptions of this highly respected trio with characters who express in their natures the changing world of late Medieval England. They tend to be interested more in profit and worldly success than in contributing to a moral society. An even starker contrast is that some of them are irreverent, fraudulent and scurrilous. The Knight, Squire and Yeoman seem on the other hand to have been pictured from a past or passing age; a Medieval England that was once romantic, chivalric and noble. The descriptions seem even to exaggerate these characters. The qualifying adjectives and adverbs do this for The Knight. On occasions these terms become 'hyperboles' (exaggerations): *no man ferre* (48) and *He nevere yet no vileynye ne sayde* (70).

The colourful description of The Squire's appearance: *Al ful of fresshe floures, whyte and reede* (90), and the joyful natural imagery: *He was as fressh as is the month of May* (92), or *He sleep namoore than dooth a nyghtyngale* (98), lend to The Squire his character of romantic, lusty youthfulness. And the full and detailed account of The Yeoman's outdoor skills: *Of wodecraft wel koude he al the usage* (110), suggests a servant on whose skills and abilities his commanders, i.e. The Knight and The Squire, could implicitly rely.

There have been suggestions that The Knight's crusades may have involved him in violent mercenary behaviour bordering on butchery, (see Notes p. 32) but there is no question mark in the text against either his or his companions' worthiness. They are, each at their own social level and within their spheres of activity, immensely successful. They also possess a surplus of the skills needed to carry out their duties. This enthusiastic and idealized outlook on a changing feudal society is never repeated. As you study the descriptions of the other pilgrims, take note of the references to affairs of the land which suggest that the Golden Age of Chivalry may well have been giving way to a new Golden Age of Commerce. Look at The Reeve in this respect, a sort of bailiff who took charge of an estate. He too possesses skills in abundance to carry out his duties:

> Ther koude no man brynge hym in arrerage.
> Ther nas baillif, ne hierde, nor oother hyne,
> That he ne knew his sleighte and his covyne;   (602–4)

But what were his main concerns and what was he most skilful at?

In the portraits of the other pilgrims it is difficult to find again the same tone of respect that Chaucer offers The Knight, Squire and Yeoman. (However good The Reeve was at managing his estate, we cannot help noticing that he was a *sclendre colerik man* (587) who made people afraid and that he always brought up the rear on the journey, so he might have been anti-social.)

But does this mean that the chivalric trio of Knight, Squire and Yeoman are the characters whom Chaucer would most esteem? Are there others who, even with their shortcomings, Chaucer admires? Is that a different kind of admiration to the sort he has for the first trio?

What is noticeable is that in the first three descriptions there is no mention of money or material gain. The main drives of the chivalric characters contrast markedly with the outright materialism of many of the others, later described. Are there other characters for whom money means nothing? You may find it helpful to read again the Notes on page 63 for the reference to Paul Strohm's suggestion in his book, *Social Chaucer*, that there is a contrast between old medieval values of lasting obligation with new standards of short-term contracts which do not bind characters in any enduring relationships. Do you find the themes of binding loyalty and service strong amongst

The Knight, Squire and Yeoman? Incidentally, these could be further categories that you might use in the Activity on p. 80: i.e. those obligated to others through duty, contrasted with those whose connections were affected by gain or loss of business and profit.

Materialism in the Secular World

Chaucer's world was complex. London, the focal point, was a place of paradox: it resounded with the construction of churches and palaces proclaiming the glory of God and of man; it was the arena for ruthless political manouvres, bitter trade dissentions and wide-scale suffering caused by inhumanity, poverty and disease.

('Chaucer and Fourteenth Century Society', Clair C. Olson, p. 32)

London was in a class of its own: the only medieval English town with a population probably in excess of 50,000 in the late Fourteenth century. It was an entrepot for the kingdom, a terminal of the Baltic, North Sea and Mediterranean trades: it attracted immigrants from the Home Counties and East Anglia, and especially from the East Midlands; and its suburbs were creeping up towards Westminster. No less than in the countryside these changes unsettled life in a number of towns, whose burgess oligarchies strove to maintain their control in a changing world. The landowners of England thus strove to counter the economic crisis, but it was often at the price of straining relations with an increasingly assertive peasantry and established urban communities.

(*The Oxford Illustrated History of Britain*, Ralph Griffiths, ed. K. D. Morgan, p. 190)

No period of history is ever characterized by one mood. Like many other periods of change, the late Fourteenth century was a varied one. However, there was a marked growth in economic life and this may have been accompanied by avariciousness and materialism which certainly Chaucer reflects in the characteristics of a number of his pilgrims. The latter part of this section looks at how this money-grabbing instinct had affected the Church, but for the moment we are concerned with the secular world of trade and industry, and the effects it was having on society.

With varying degrees of irony and indignation, Geoffrey Chaucer reminds us in a number of the portraits how a love of money and the lifestyles associated with wealth are strong factors which motivate the behaviour of a new and emerging class of men in a bustling urban world.

Profit lies at the heart of activities in trade, industry and commerce as many of the pilgrims seek to make a living, honestly or otherwise, in a newly developing economic society. These are characters such as The Guildsmen, The Merchant, The Doctor of Physic and The Manciple. Chaucer shows that their profit motive and their quests for status affect their whole characters and not simply those features of their lives connected with professional tasks.

Connections between a love of profit and other character traits arise in ironic and amusing ways. The Merchant's (p. 9) elegant and neat appearance, his bearing on his horse and his rather pompous obsession with advertising the value of his own profits, all conceal the possibility that he may be heavily in debt. His operations in a money market show that he is involved in the beginnings of a capitalist money lending system. (See Notes pp. 46–7.) Success could bring great wealth and attendant social esteem, but these were activities fraught with danger, and the risks of bankruptcy were high. Do you find a contrast between his elegant appearance and proud bearing and his rather shaky financial circumstances?

Chaucer's ironic dismissal of the man: *But, sooth to seyn, I noot how men hym calle* (284) suggests just this tension between success and failure. The earlier pompous nature of the description is completely undercut by his anonymity.

A similar thing happens in the portrait of The Sergeant of the Law. (p. 10) He too gives an appearance of influential activity in his business as a purchaser of land. Here is a character of very considerable qualities, appointed by the King to be a Justice of the Peace, dignified in his appearance and respected for his knowledge, and yet he too is cut down to size by Chaucer as *he semed bisier than he was* (322).

The pride of the Guildsmen, all of whom possess both property and income, is partly given expression through the ambitiousness of their wives for whom it would be *ful fair to been ycleped 'madame,'* (376) should their husbands aspire to the office of aldermen.

For others the poem expresses more directly the connections

between profit motive and personality trait. The Shipman is an unscrupulous thief and smuggler, and The Doctor of Physic unashamedly keeps all the money which accrues to him in times of plague: *He kepte that he wan in pestilence* (442). The Miller was a clever thief and swindler: *Wel koude he stelen corn and tollen thries;* (562) and The Manciple was so clever in the dealings he had with his masters in the Inns of Court that he was able to swindle them all.

Activity

People's attitudes towards profit, wealth, and indeed to self-denial and poverty, are often revealed in other characteristics that they possess. Consider carefully the group of 'mercantile-class' pilgrims in the light of this statement. Define each one's financial situation and his attitude towards money. Can you find other characteristics which tell us something about the links between their personalities and their professional behaviour? Always remember to supply close evidence from the text.

Discussion

Chaucer's capacity to see through his characters and to reveal their basic motives is never so strong as when he is dealing with those inwardly affected by the profit motive. The power of wealth is tenacious. To describe its hold on some of the characters he uses some strong imagery. For example, The Doctor of Physic, well-practised in the science of the medical profession, is given health and happiness through his delight in profit:

> For gold in phisik is a cordial,
> Therefore he lovede gold in special. (443–4)

The Miller, a dishonest scoundrel, steals grain and takes his toll for it three times over. His love of profit is brought out in a vivid metaphor:

> And yet he hadde a thombe of gold, pardee. (563)

In addition to imagery, Chaucer represents self-important and ambitious characters with heightened realism through descriptions of their tone of voice and their appearance. The Merchant is *Sownynge* (275) always on the subject of his profits; there is a vivid impression of The

Doctor of Physic delaying his patients *In houres by his magyk natureel*; (416) and The Guildsmen appear with their lavish equipment beautifully mounted and adorned (365–8).

Any age produces its barterers and traffickers, hagglers and hucksters, and perhaps too any age its quota of thieves and scoundrels. In the *General Prologue* there are a few direct references to these sorts of dealings. Do we learn anything about the conscience of a smuggler when we are told that The Shipman took no account of his enemies but unceremoniously threw them overboard in a fight? And does the daunting appearance of The Miller make it more or less surprising that he should steal corn?

But love of money is not restricted to the thieving of The Miller or smuggling of The Shipman. Chaucer reveals others as characters whose personalities have become wholly affected by the prospects of profit and social advance, although their self-image may mean that they see and think of themselves as upright and important professional members of society. This can happen through chance comments which may need a second glance for their fullest importance.

What significance is there in the way The Merchant wears his boots, The Guildsmen their apparel, and The Doctor of Physic his colourful coat?

Even if Chaucer seems economical with the truth about their financial dealings, there is often enough in the descriptions of the appearances, and behaviour, of these characters to reveal the truth of their avaricious, pompous and fraudulent natures. It is not untypical of Chaucer's style, however, for him to be just a little wary of revealing the full truth about dishonest dealings. Does this style of understatement make the characters seem more or less avaricious? What other motives do you think Chaucer may have had for being so careful with what he said?

The Materialistic Outlook of the Church

The Church was also interested in money. At times the poem suggests that its officials were driven almost entirely by greed and avarice, although The Parson (p. 15) and Ploughman (p.16) are, by contrast, models of frugal behaviour, uncorrupted and driven only by a desire to please God, unrewarded through their work. But they are exceptional. It is worthwhile thinking about what makes them so different in order to understand just how corrupt some of the other church characters have become. The Parson displays in his humble generosity a trait the opposite of any profit motive:

> But rather wolde he yeven, out of doute,
> Unto his povre parisshens aboute
> Of his offryng and eek of his substaunce.   (487–9)

And his ploughman-brother worked the land:

> For Cristes sake, for every povre wight,
> Withouten hire, if it lay in his myght.   (537–8)

These two singular examples are contrasted with a succession of money-grabbing approaches to life from the other ecclesiastics. And remember these were the very people whose dealings with the population should, by all law and conscience, have been governed less by a desire to extort advantage and more by the need to impose moral authority. The Friar most resembles the mercantile characters in his efforts to achieve social status; he would prefer to keep company with innkeepers, barmaids and local merchants of victuals, rather than lower himself in the eyes of the community through association with lepers and beggars.

Activity

What evidence can you find of the wealth and avarice of the Church characters? What ironic evidence is there that they perform their ecclesiastical duties well?

Discussion

You could select examples of avarice from The Friar (p. 7) and The Pardoner (p. 20). The Monk (p. 6) is also worth considering (his clothes alone suggest surely that he must have been well off!) and so is The Summoner (p. 19).

Think about the ironic descriptions of characters whose ability to perform their righteous and rightful tasks was exemplary – what were their real motives for performing their ecclesiastical duties so well?

You will need to think about such matters as The Monk's dress (193–5); why was The Friar's '*In Principio*' (254) so pleasant?; what contradictions were there in The Summoner's attitude towards excommunication (654–5); how did The Pardoner treat poor parsons? (701–4).

Evidence of Avarice in the Church

How typical was this taste for wealth and well-being in the medieval Church? Muriel Bowden in *A Commentary on the General Prologue to The Canterbury Tales*, has discovered numerous references to the state of avaricious hypocrisy amongst contemporaries of Chaucer's characters. She quotes from Gower, another medieval writer, who complained of monks in his *Mirour de l'Omme*:

> The monk of the present day wears a habit which is a beautiful adornment to the body, and for vain honour he is clad in a furred cloak. Let the monk be filled with consternation who makes himself handsome for the world, who wears the finest wool furred with costly grey squirrel rather than a hair shirt!

Here is another revealing quotation from Thomas Wright's collection of medieval *Political Poems*. An honest ploughman has this to say about monks he knew:

> Some wearen mitre and ring,
> With double worsted well ydight,
> With royall meat and rich drinke,
> And rideth on a courser as a knight.

Gower, a much more orthodox Christian than Geoffrey Chaucer, wrote of the Franciscan Order:

> The Friars preach of poverty yet they always have an open hand to receive riches. They have perverted their Order from within by their covetousness. They wish ease, but they will not labour – in no case do they do their duty.

Summoners were regularly attacked in political poems, often in contempt for doing the business of avaricious bishops or archdeacons, who, again in Wright's words, *cared for neither right nor wrong if they smell a bribe*. In fact the extortionate behaviour of summoners was the subject of a parliamentary plea, dated 1378:

And also the said Summoners make their summons to diverse people for malice when they are going in their carts to the fields and elsewhere, and these extortioners impute crimes to the poor, contriving that the poor shall pay a fine which is called the Bishope Almois; or else the said Summoners demand that the people appear for trial twenty or more leagues from their homes, sometimes to two places on one day, to the great dis-ease, impoverishment, and oppression of the said poor Commons. It is begged that Parliament consider these great harms.

The Church contributed directly to the potential for dishonesty amongst pardoners. These were often vagabonds rather than the genuine churchmen who would have been authorized to buy and sell relics from Rome in order to offer redemption and salvation to sinners who repented and confessed. The practice was inevitably ripe for corruption: indulgences were forged and pardons were sold without any question of a proper confession. The Pope himself – Boniface IX – aware of the widespread malpractice, charged in a papal edict of 1390 that henceforth all pardoners be made to vow that they come fully authorized from Rome.

Other Failings in the Ecclesiastical Characters

The characters from the Church have other failings as well as materialism and avarice, although the profit motive does appear to lie at the heart of the breakdown in its moral authority.

No group of characters more fully represents the contrast in the poem between expectation and reality of calling. From the descriptions of the very pilgrims whose vocations should have been devout responses to their holy duties, we gather a distinct impression that all was not as it should have been with the practices of the medieval Church as it carried out its moral, legal, social and financial duties. But a degree of corruption is perhaps hardly surprising. There is, after all, ample evidence from many of the other pilgrims that profit and wealth were important goals in the life of late medieval society, and the Church, no less than other landowners, was involved in daily dealings with the mass of people. Increasingly the financial and legal affairs of Church officials were routine activities as important as its pastoral ones. Because it was a land owner, and due to a long tradition, the Church exacted tithes. It also made money for its own institutions and, as we see so clearly in the practice of The Summoner, undertook judicial tasks such as the summoning of offenders, both moral and secular, to court.

Chaucer's description of The Parson expresses how, ideally, the duties of the Church should have been carried out. This diligent parish priest, who tramped in all weathers on foot about his entire parish, his staff symbolically held in his hand, and who genuinely lived by the law of Christ *and his apostles twelve* (527), exemplified in his own personal devotion to high moral standards the values he expected in others. But he was unique. His literal obedience of Christ's law contrasts with the lack of religious observance in the others. It has even been suggested that one purpose of such a devout portrait is criticism of those who are false to the Church's true values.

The violations of Christian doctrine elsewhere leave an overall impression of hypocrisy, worldliness and corruption. However, Chaucer's exposure of the Church is not always intended to condemn the characters who represent it. Some of the worldliness and personal vitality in The Monk and The Friar are qualities he seems positively to admire. He is also conscious of the considerable clerical and secular skills possessed by this group, even when they are put to use hypocritically or perversely. What is he suggesting when he tells us, for example, of The Friar that *plesaunt was his absolucioun* (222) and that The Pardoner was a *noble ecclesiaste* (708)? At times it seems that the more corrupt the purpose of the Church characters, the more accomplished is their use of ecclesiastical practices and skills.

Chaucer appears to hold an ambiguous view of The Monk (*a fair for the maistrie*, [165]). He warms to his philosophy of abandoning the old Benedictine rule as too restrictive. On the other hand his love of hunting and sport, activities which may have been disloyal to the orders of his monastery, and his wealthy and elaborate appearance, make him a very worldly character. But how harsh is Chaucer's tone? Are there things about The Monk which Chaucer admires?

The Friar is exposed possibly as a greater hypocrite. How skilful are his deceptions? He has considerable powers of language, is gratifying in confession and graciously humble when most it suits him. In the same ironic way that The Pardoner is a *noble ecclesiaste* (708), he is a *worthy lymytour* (269), even if his professional intentions are not, truly, *so vertuous* (251).

In spite of their hypocrisy, the vitality of The Monk and The Friar may be admired by Chaucer – some critics have suggested that dynamic human vitality is a theme of the poem – especially when we compare them with the sombre description of The Clerk (p. 9). He may be a man who genuinely prays for the souls of his benefactors, but presents to the world an aloof and unexciting appearance which Chaucer hardly admires. In a striking comparison with The Monk, who:

> . . yaf nat of that text a pulled hen,
> That seith that hunters ben nat hooly men,
> Ne that a monk, when he is recchelees,
> Is likned til a fissh that is waterlees...   (177–80)

The Clerk has the works of Aristotle for learned reference and inspiration, at the head of his bed. Are similar comparisons possible between lines describing The Friar and The Parson?

Including The Prioress (who will be discussed in greater detail on p. 111), you will notice that the first set of ecclesiastical pilgrims comes across as slightly misplaced and unorthodox as far as Church doctrine is concerned, but commonplace in the world at large. They are rule-breakers, certainly, but hardly condemned by Chaucer's mild irony. And the emphasis on so many of their skills and accomplishments suggests that in their relations with others, not necessarily Church brethren, their codes of behaviour would be accepted as down-to-earth and natural. So far, it is really only The Friar who gives cause for moral concern because of his accomplished avarice.

Activity

How does the tone change for the descriptions of The Summoner (p. 19) and The Pardoner (p. 20)? What techniques does Chaucer use to reveal their characters? How do their physical characteristics and appearances add to our impressions of their immoral conduct?

Discussion

Corruption waits till the last. As if finally to assert his moral credentials, just as he starts with the most noble and honourable of men, The

Knight, Chaucer saves his sharpest invective for the most immoral of Church characters: The Summoner and The Pardoner. Physically The Summoner is also the most loathsome of the company.

They are reprehensible but we have possibly been prepared for the worst in human nature in the rough but ready Miller and the fearsome Reeve.

Both The Summoner and The Pardoner, as we have seen, worked in readily corruptible positions. Do you think it is their offices or their personalities that Chaucer wants to expose and condemn? Look at the vivid character assassination that takes place on The Summoner. What is Chaucer telling us about him in the section starting at line 635 as he describes his behaviour when drunk? What do we think of a man who exhausted the extent of his learning so quickly and spoke language like the mimicry of a parrot? How does his dismissal of the power of excommunication compare with The Parson's attitude to sinners (*What so he were, of heigh or lough estat,* [522]). Chaucer is unusually rude about The Summoner's appearance. Does he intend a connection between his ugly looks and his powers of corruption?

Consider the irony which is used to describe The Pardoner's false eloquence as a preacher. What effect would he have had on his congregations? And is there further comparison to be made with The Parson's:

> Wel oghte a preest ensample for to yive,
> By his clennesse, how that his sheep sholde lyve. (505–6)

Part of Chaucer's art lies in his capacity to express corruption in lines of personal appearance. This undoubtedly happens with The Summoner. Does the same happen with The Pardoner? What impression do you get of The Pardoner's character from the description of his apparent effeminacy and the image he has of himself riding *al of the newe jet* (682) – in the latest fashion? What might they have thought of his audacity in the way he tries to sell indulgences? If you had been one of the pilgrims why might you have been wary of him? Is he simply a detestable rogue or are there characteristics in his behaviour, which, as with The Friar, we might find impressive? These are the kinds of questions which will help you come to a decision as to just how evil he was.

Food, Drink, and Greet Chiere

Frequent reference to food and drink offers further insight into medieval society. Gluttony is also established as part of the theme of indulgence and the pursuit of self-interest.

Many of the more indulgent characters may have spent the entire evening eating and drinking throughout the course of the *General Prologue*. They were being well looked after in the Tabard by the hospitable Host. There is a cheery atmosphere, aided by strong wine: *Strong was the wyn, and wel to drynke us leste.* (750).

The Host's character is revealed through his dialogue and actions, but there is a brief account of the man who resembles in some ways The Monk, The Franklin and The Guildsmen:

> A large man he was with eyen stepe—
> A fairer burgeys was ther noon in Chepe—
> Boold of his speche, and wys, and wel ytaught,
> And of manhod hym lakkede right naught.   (753–6)

This perceptiveness, manliness and wordly wisdom are soon, as we see from his challenge, to be turned to opportunism. He has fed the company well and they have drunk strong wine. He then appears to have little difficulty persuading the pilgrims – effectively his customers – to agree to his proposal. As has been suggested in the Notes (p. 74) he will be assured of another healthy night's business. We learn a great deal more of this genial character during the interludes to the tales themselves; he acts as a kind of master of ceremonies, orchestrating the story-telling with careful control, intervening in squabbles and keeping everybody happy.

The Tabard with its roomy chambers and stables was likely to have been a superior inn. The Host would have been responsible for the conduct of all guests under his roof; he would have had to remove their arms for safe-keeping and ensure that they did not venture out after curfew; there would have been restrictions on what food and drink he could make on the premises and he would have been restricted with fixed charges on his tariff. Does this background to the work of innkeepers help us to understand Harry Baily's character? (The name of the man is revealed in *The Cook's Prologue*).

There are a number of other references to the eating and drinking habits of the pilgrims. The vivid account of The Prioress's table manners helps to detail her flourishing courtliness:

> Hir over-lippe wyped she so clene
> That in hir coppe ther was no ferthyng sene
> Of grece, whan she dronken hadde hir draughte.
> Ful semely after hir mete she raughte. (133–6)

The possibility is that Chaucer based these lines on a remarkably similar passage from the *Roman de la Rose* in which a woman was using her elegant and fastidious table manners to be attractive to her lover. (See Appendix, p. 150.)

The indulgent Monk, who loved hunting, is provided in his description with what is surely one of the most succulent lines in literature: *A fat swan loved he best of any roost.* (206).

The Friar associated with franklins, preferring their genial company to that of beggars and lepers, whose plight should have consumed more of his time. We are told that his preference was to deal *al with riche and selleres of vitaille.* (248).

The underfed Clerk contrasts with the more gluttonous pilgrims. This gaunt Oxford scholar is rather similar in build to his equally emaciated horse:

> As leene was his hors as is a rake,
> And he nas nat right fat, I undertake,
> But looked holwe, and therto sobrely. (287–9)

Clearly a decent meal in the Tabard would have done him nothing but good! Do you think the frugality of The Clerk contrasts with the gluttony of others?

Indulgence is evident in the description of The Franklin. This successful landowner, who has been a member of parliament, is another one who lives life to the full, like The Monk and Friar. He also resembles The Wife of Bath. Like her, he was capable of losing his temper rather severely; we are told how cross he could become with his cook (351–2). His epicurean philosophy led him to believe *that pleyn delit / Was verray felicitee parfit.* (337–8), pure pleasure being the sign of a life of perfect happiness.

Activity

What does Chaucer mean when he describes The Franklin as *sangwyn*? (See Note to line 333 (p. 51) which explains the humours by which it was assumed that medieval people were governed.)

How does hyperbole (exaggeration) and imagery establish the indulgent character of The Franklin? Do you get the impression of an indulgent age from the descriptions of other characters? What other forms of indulgent behaviour are present in addition to gluttony?

Discussion

When you consider other forms of indulgence it will be worth thinking again about the behaviour of some of the Church characters, and also look at the discussion that follows on the two women (p. 110) especially The Wife of Bath. Remember that the poem was modelled on the Estates Satire, so that many of the characters are depicted as falling short of the ideal to which each should have conformed. Perhaps one way of looking at this is that they were tempted to indulge in pleasures which distracted them from their true moral and socially expected courses in life.

A little understanding of medieval feasting might also help you to see that characters such as The Franklin (p. 10) were not out of the ordinary. In spite of the vulnerability of the poor to famine and plague, many landowners and wealthy people in the late Fourteenth century were, by contrast, living very satisfying lives. It is clear that The Franklin arranges things so that food and drink in his household are not merely a matter of sustenance but available for a permanent feast. He had changed the earlier medieval practice of taking down the trestle table between meals, leaving it permanently in place in his hall:

His table dormant in his halle alway
Stood redy covered al the longe day. (353–4)

A medieval feast would have been a truly sumptuous affair. See illustration from Luttrell Psalter on p. 128. Muriel Bowden in *A Commentary on the General Prologue to The Canterbury Tales*, listed a first course of brawn with mustard, bacon and peas; beef and boiled chickens (boiling was a popular method of cooking meat in the Middle Ages), roast goose, capon and a richly made dish of pastries stuffed with cream, eggs, vegetables, fruit and spices. This would invariably have been followed by a rich stew of meat or fish and more stuffed pastries; then thin slices of fried bread; apples and pears if they were in season; and finally bread, and cheese with spiced cakes or wafers. If this was the kind of diet that Chaucer had in mind in The Franklin's household, the famous metaphor of 'it snowing meat and drink' seems highly appropriate.

The theme of epicurean indulgence does not end with The Franklin. The Guildsmen (p. 11) have decided to take their own cook on the pilgrimage with them. We have already had hints of the preoccupations of many of the other pilgrims as they assemble for this most holy of journeys. What does this decision of The Guildsmen reveal of their most pressing concerns as they set out? Their accompanying cook is afforded a brief description in his own right. This allows Chaucer a further opportunity to show off his knowledge of culinary activities – how spices were used, the various means of cooking meat, and how to make a good hash or *blankmanger* (387) – all of which presents yet another character whose skills are hyperbolically presented as amongst the best (*For blankmanger, that made he with the beste* (387). How does Chaucer combine his knowledge of The Cook's skills with the themes of gluttony and self-indulgence? What kind of life has The Cook been leading?

The Two Women

The only two descriptions of female characters, The Prioress (p. 4) and The Wife of Bath (p. 14) , are celebrated examples of irony and humour. One of the most notable features of Chaucer's irony is that his characters are often at their most assertive, their skills and accomplishments at their best when their true motives for the kinds of lives they lead are most in opposition to what might be expected of them. This certainly happens with The Prioress and Wife of Bath. The Prioress is a nun presented in a detailed style suggesting her wholehearted concern with courtly elegance. The Wife of Bath is a formidable cloth-maker presented in a robust style which calls into question the motives for her pilgrimage.

The accounts reveal the vanity and aspirations of the two women. They also raise some of the poem's powerful issues about the nature of the human condition: is it in the nature of human life that people become most strongly motivated by a need for esteem and recognition?

There is some dispute as to the extent of Chaucer's irony in the portrait of The Prioress, but there is little doubting the fact that he intended her femininity as if she were the heroine of a medieval romance in the disguise of an ecclesiastical calling. Her studied singing, the French she spoke, her meticulous table manners, sympathetic treatment of small animals and her elegantly adorned mode of dress all suggest a benign person but one who has been practising the modesty and quiet demeanour of so many of the heroines of courtly romance. Madame Eglentyne's name itself – hers by choice – is more likely to have originated from a character in a romance than from one modelled on religious life. The stock phrase *symple and coy* (119) denotes the kind of quiet but possibly seductive modesty of the courtly romance heroine. There are numerous details of her physical appearance such as her shapely nose (*tretys* [152]), sparkling eyes (*greye as glas* [152]), small, soft, red mouth and her fair forehead, which, however broad it was, should not even have been uncovered. Part of the irony arises because the traits in her character do suggest virtuous behaviour, such as modesty, charity, pity, and generosity, but not that this devotion is motivated by her duty to God. Why would a courtly heroine behave in such a pleasant and attractive manner?

Courtly love as a tradition meant that love was almost a specialized art. The male lover would be a humble person, obedient to his intended lady's slightest wish. He would often have to tolerate rejection of his advances. Sometimes women would delight in making themselves unattainable. This would mean that, if their affection could finally be won, they would be prized more valuably. Thus, love was rather like the feudal society: just as dependents on the land had to do service to their lord, so the lover was a kind of slave to his lady. Because of this, the activity of 'wooing' was a polite, courteous and reverential type of behaviour.

The Wife of Bath is less modest about the need to establish a status in her community. In the parish of St Michael-juxta-Bathon, the cloth industry flourished, and here, as was the case elsewhere in Medieval England, women were prominent in its pursuit. As well as being a prominent woman in the parish, she was also assertive and dominant. If the Prioress was motivated to behave quietly and modestly in a courtly manner in order to satisfy her vanity, The Wife of Bath showed no similar sense of reserve or decorum. There is a lack of shame in all that she does: as she insists on being the first at the altar; in the ostentatious clothing she wears; and in her willingness to be so frank about her past.

Study the characteristics of The Wife of Bath. In the first instance, if she was deaf, would this tend to draw attention to her or allow her to merge into the background? In her use of skills at weaving, she is described as superior to those in the major European cloth-making centres of Ypres and Ghent. But, if Chaucer has only briefly made her acquaintance, whose view of her expertise is this? Has she told him? And so soon? Given her determination and competitiveness for priority at the offertory, how would she behave if ever denied such a status? After reading the lines:

> ...certeyn so wrooth was she
> That she was out of alle charitee. (451–2)

do we understand just how angry she would be if so crossed?

What does her clothing on Sundays reveal about her personality, and why do you think Chaucer decides to give an estimate of the weight of her *coverchiefs* (453–5)?

She has had considerable and varied sexual experience: five husbands, even without mentioning *oother compaignye in youthe* (461), a hint of lechery on her previous pilgrimages and profound knowledge of cures for love-sickness and tricks of the trade in the business of love and sex (*For she koude of that art the olde daunce* [476]). Alongside The Squire, therefore, she links most directly with the interest aroused in a sensual response to life in the opening lines of the poem. For a woman so proud, flamboyant and overbearing, how well prepared do you think she is for the pilgrimage? Is there evidence that her ambitions are pointing in other directions as she sets off to the tomb of the *hooly blisful martir* (17)?

Activity

Do you agree that vanity is a characteristic of The Prioress and Wife of Bath? Which other characters are vain? Can you suggest evidence of vain behaviour?

Discussion

Of course, a number of the male characters also exhibit signs of vanity in their personal and professional affairs: The Sergeant of the Law does, The Guildsmen do as they seek the office of aldermen (although interestingly Chaucer does point out that this would satisfy the vanity of their wives). And like The Wife of Bath, many of the men seek to control their lives and the lives of others in the world about them: The Manciple has this trait, as does The Reeve. So what are the differences that are brought out specifically in the lives of the two women?

Both descriptions, with different points of emphasis, reveal attitudes towards women in the Middle Ages. The Prioress, who would initially have been elected to be the head of her convent, with the approval of her bishop, would partly have been presiding over an order that had received an endowment and partly overseeing that it was a going concern in the community. Just like a well-to-do woman in the town or countryside, her job would have been to supervise the property of the convent – its farms, its stables, its fields, – not unlike the role of The Reeve in fact. Many prioresses were highly respected in their communities, enjoying the same privileges as lords of manors.

Although many prioresses were never distracted from the strictness and austerity of their vows, which required contemplative isolation from the fashions and influences of the secular world, others, because of their contact with the outside, were very worldly – a characteristic explored also in The Monk and The Friar. If The Monk's worldliness is indeed a highly masculine response to life: hunting, gaming, sporting and drinking; the Prioress's is intensively and coquettishly feminine. Her secular approach to life is based on an impression she has of herself taking part in the peace-time activities of courtly love. Her intricate, detailed and very self-conscious behaviour was a fastidious imitation of the sort of noblewoman who, in many a great medieval household, would have occupied herself with enriching the cultural and literary lives of the nobility, and have drawn attention to herself as a potential lover for male suitors diverted from military service. Such men, with time and leisure on their hands, would have been intent on proving their prowess in the struggles of love and courtship.

What we learn of The Wife of Bath is more overtly sexual. In addition to the subtle seductiveness of The Prioress, there are oblique references to sex elsewhere amongst the pilgrims: the young Squire who slept no more than a nightingale (98); The Friar who *hadde maad*

ful many a mariage / Of yonge wommen at his owene cost. (212–13);
The Miller who told lewd stories (560–1); and The Summoner – *As
hoot he was and lecherous as a sparwe,* (626). But nowhere is sexual
desire and drive so evident as in the past, and probably in the present
intentions, of The Wife of Bath.

A traditional view of female sexuality was that, once tempted, a
woman's true sexual nature would stand constantly revealed. In
Boccaccio's *Decameron*, also of the late Fourteenth century,
(1348–1353), there are numerous innocent sexual heroines. Once
their virginity was relinquished, they became insatiable, frequently
reducing men to a state of impotence! The *Decameron* was an earlier
Italian work, also a collection of tales, which Chaucer may have had
access to whilst in Italy.

The Wife of Bath expresses more about her controlling, but
uncontrolled, sexual urge, in her own tale and its prologue. She is a
woman of vigorous and exhausting sexual energy. As so often
happens in Chaucer's style of characterization, we learn much about
the main characteristic in her personality through its expression
elsewhere in her life. If she dominates so determinedly in her
profession as a clothier and brushes the parish aside at the altar, how
are we supposed to imagine her treatment of husbands and lovers?

Approaches through Chaucer's Poetic Technique

Structure

One of the purposes of the poem – or at least one of the results – is to
introduce the characters. What makes this unusual is that the writer
is one of them. Following the elegant poetical opening, Chaucer
admits that he is delaying the main part of the poem. He and his
companions are comfortably installed in the Tabard for the night, so,
somewhat conversationally, and certainly politely, he decides to tell
us about the other pilgrims:

> Er that I ferther in this tale pace,
> Me thynketh it acordaunt to resoun
> To telle yow al the condicioun
> Of ech of hem, so as it semed me ...   (36–9)

The structure of the poem is from then on, in some respects, more like a conversation, a sort of confidential chat with friends, rather than an example of formal poetry, although it retains many features of the latter. Throughout the descriptions of the pilgrims, this relaxed conversational style has the effect of making us feel privileged to be a party to Chaucer's observations.

Such a tête-à-tête with the reader is often marked at the beginnings and endings of the portraits. In calm undertones Chaucer passes from one character to another, frequently telling us who accompanies whom, the order of the procession and how they sit on what kind of horse, all of which may seem trivial but is another way of revealing character.

Activity
Do the references to the sorts of horses ridden, or the stances of some characters in the saddle, help to reveal characteristics of the pilgrims?

Chaucer's Own Character: the Poet

Chaucer wishes his writing to be judged humbly. But remember there is a deliberate self-consciousness about this position. Can we accept the request entirely at face value or do you think there is a kind of mischief in his words? The quiet, modest tone behind which he hides and denies his skills suggests a poet deliberately apologizing for his own shortcomings. Whilst he considers it important to describe the appearance of the pilgrims, he stresses that this will be *so as it semed me*, (39), as if toying with his readership – are we to disbelieve his perceptions or accept them as the simple truth? Does this drawing of attention to his humility enhance or diminish his credibility as a faithful reporter?

Following the portrait of The Pardoner, he feels obliged to offer a much longer apology for the language he will need to use if he is to relay the tales as they were spoken – and in the interests of truth this will include language *rudeliche and large* (734), as it will be spoken by the various story-tellers. He also puts himself down as he begs forgiveness if in his portraits he has failed to accord to each pilgrim his or her proper status in life. Have you noticed that as a failing? (Are we left with a slight feeling anyway that a tone of apology would not go amiss after what he has had to say about a number of his new friends?!) How do you react to his comments and apologies between lines 715 and 746?

Is this all just politeness or is there a cleverly constructed pose? Part of the purpose of his false modesty may be to make him appear less responsible for what is said. To what extent do you think that his reserve is just such a tactic?

The Pilgrim

Understanding the interaction between the poet and the pilgrim is a little more complicated. As you assess his reactions to what he observes in the Tabard ask yourself whether he reacts as Chaucer the Poet or as Chaucer the Pilgrim. The latter is, after all, a created character. Again, a comparison can be made with novels – of later centuries – many of which are written in the first person. Are there advantages for him if he can hide behind the character of the Pilgrim that he has created for himself?

Chaucer soon expresses a wish to be thought of as one of the company. He is quickly *of hir felaweshipe anon* (32). Neither the structure of the poem, nor indeed modesty, allow for a comparable style of portrait of the poet. However, he is able, subtly and with an apparent lack of self-consciousness, to reveal his own character. Of course there is none of the minute detail of appearance or physique that we get with the other pilgrims, but there are just enough hints of the image he has of his own skills as a writer and occasional glimpses of his own opinions:

And I seyde his opinion was good. (183)

There is also a strong impression of his intelligence and perceptiveness, and, perhaps above all these, an emerging picture of his moral code and philosophy. But do you also detect a superior air about him when he passes comment, as he does in the above reference to The Monk's attitudes? He can be very dismissive, as with the anonymity of The Merchant and with the way he mocks the apparent preoccupations of The Sergeant of the Law. What conclusion can you draw from his comment on the fact that The Prioress spoke French, not in the fashion of the royal court but *After the scole of Stratford atte Bowe?* (125).

Activity

Try writing a portrait of Chaucer himself – The Poet. You could do this in either prose or poetry! Do it in Middle English if you prefer – it may be a good way of helping you to understand how the language works!

Discussion

It will be difficult to include a physical description of Chaucer, but you should be able to find evidence of his outlook on life in order to make an assessment of his character.

He is conscious of social status: is it simply coincidence that he should say:

And at a knyght than wol I first bigynne. (42)

We have repeatedly discovered him to be worldly, knowledgeable and even learned; sometimes this encourages him to a degree of showiness, perhaps a trait he is willing to mock in himself. He has a sense of perspective; he can laugh gently at the less harmful failings in human beings and ridicule those which exert a more dangerous influence. Above all, Geoffrey Chaucer comes across as an enthusiast. He admires the abundant qualities through which his fellow human beings show their love of human life.

Whatever the advantages, you may find that there are some traits which dominate the personality of the man behind the pilgrim Chaucer. There are lots of qualities which appeal to him: the youthful vitality of The Squire; The Monk's love of the good things in life; the hospitality of The Franklin and the professional skills of The Yeoman, The Shipman, and The Doctor of Physic; the elaborate deception of The Prioress and the lustiness of The Wife of Bath. He seems fascinated with the inherent quality in the approaches to life of The Knight, The Parson and Ploughman; he has an envious appreciation of the opportunism and *joie de vivre* in The Host – and all of these contrast with his expression of the negative forces in The Reeve, The Summoner and The Pardoner. It is hard to believe that these reactions are not his own.

Elsewhere, admittedly, he may have had to pass quickly over the avarice of The Friar, the hypocrisy of The Merchant, the temper of The Franklin and the crimes of The Shipman and Miller, but in reality none of these failings quite matches his derision of the last trio: a Reeve whose cunning and insect-like features repulse people; The Summoner whose scaly physical appearance is matched only by the slippery ignorance of his frightening behaviour; and finally The Pardoner, who may be the cleverest of his kind but is intentionally a swindler.

> But of his craft, fro Berwyk into Ware
> Ne was ther swich another pardoner; (692–3)

Can you see how the pose in the narrative stance might come to Chaucer's aid? Who do we blame for his questionable tolerance of some of the hypocrisy? Is it the Pilgrim or the Poet?

Style

One reason why a variety of styles is needed is because of Chaucer's window on such a range of characters drawn from so many walks of life and from different social classes. How does his language cope with such a variety of class backgrounds: with, for example, the chivalry of The Knight and courtliness of The Prioress at one end of the social scale and the ditch-digging of The Ploughman and lewd buffoonery of The Miller at the other?

It is probably fruitless either to identify or classify all the stylistic devices in the poem – this would have the effect of killing dead the spontaneity and unexpectedness of so much of the language. But there are some features which stand out. Many of these have already been mentioned in the discussions of individual portraits. Look for the use of hyperbole or exaggeration: so many of the pilgrims are the best, unsurpassed or incomparable in what they do. Even if these descriptions of human skill and achievement are sometimes damning and ironic, they do seem to suggest over and over again Chaucer's delight in the power of human achievement.

Consider the way that a dominant trait is often identified, around which other features of character are constructed, and related to the dominant characteristic: for The Knight, his worthiness; The Prioress, her courtliness; The Miller, his brawn, etc. This may result in an understanding of characteristics of the type of person (or Estate) and also serves to offer insight into the behaviour of the character as an individual.

Look for examples of realism; the language of the farmyard and the kitchen used just as well as that of the court and crusade. This realistic approach has been termed 'familiarity' or 'provincialism'. At times it is very colloquial, commonly in imagery (look at the image he uses to stress the exemplary approach to life given by The Parson to his flock [500]).

He uses both metaphor and simile, but he does at times appear more at ease with simile as a literary device, almost as if his images need to be drawn out in natural conversation, (e.g. The Monk: *his brydel heere / Gynglen... as dooth the chapel belle* [169–71]; The Clerk: *As leene was his hors as is a rake,* [287]). Can you at times see the emergence of another kind of realism when, for example, the tone and intonation of a pilgrim's voice is suggested? Or when the punctuation, the enjambement and the onomatopoeia give an impression of a character's actions. In these respects you might notice how The Wife of Bath's complexion suggests a breathless hustle and busyness; how well the lines to describe The Parson suggest something of his tireless trudge into the corners of his parish; how vividly we visualize the Ploughman at his willing toil as: *He wolde thresshe, and therto dyke and delve,* (536); or how easy it becomes to imagine the stoutly-built Miller breaking down the door *at a rennyng* (551).

An earlier section of this book has referred to Chaucer's impressive attempts to display knowledge through the feature of style sometimes termed 'encyclopaedism'. This can have the effect of lending a deliberate doctrinal air to the work. It is a style he returns to again and again in the tales in order to provide 'exemplar' – catalogues of argument to strengthen the authority of the speaker. A similar device is the 'inventory'. This involves a list of characteristics, such as personal features, complexion, physique, dress, apparel, tools of a trade, all of which offer not just a physical impression of the pilgrims but indicate character as well, and of course contribute to their individuality. This tendency to take stock of a character originated in the high style of French romances which Chaucer consciously used as a model for his art.

Irony

The unifying mixture of styles – the calm juxtaposition of a conventional, high literary style with the realism of everyday life – allows Chaucer the constant possibility of satirizing his characters. Their pedestals can quickly be knocked from under their feet, their self-importance reduced to ironic farce, and when necessary, their immorality crushingly exposed. In addition to exposing shortcomings of types of character as in Estates Satire, Chaucer displays a sharply perceptive awareness of human nature.

Is the main subject of the poem – i.e. pilgrimage – treated ironically? The nature of the pilgrimage calls into question the assertion that many of these pilgrims would be in the saddle with *ful devout corage*, (22). Many of them, we assume, will be failing in their hearts and minds to aspire to a holy state of readiness for their task ahead. Their journey will be a diversion rather than a contemplation.

Activity

Look carefully at the ending of the poem: the long section from line 747. If you were looking on at the start of this merry company's journey, say as another guest or a servant in the Tabard, what sort of impressions would you form of this, the start of a holy journey?

Discussion

An enduring interpretation of the characters is that of self-interest. As you have seen there are honourable exceptions, but frankly as they ride *Unto the Wateryng of Seint Thomas* (826), we are left with a distinct impression of a group of people who are, one way or another, 'on the make', or at the very least using pilgrimage as pleasure, contemplation as recreation, devotion as diversion.

Yet this is not to suggest that Chaucer sets out to judge all his characters nor condemn all their behaviour. His ambivalent attitude to the self-denial of The Clerk and his enthusiasm for the vigour of The

Monk remind us that Chaucer's own outlook on life was far from austere. His irony and mockery are at times mild, showing us merely that the motivations of human beings are complex and their personalities full of contradictions, many of which are comic. But even though he may poke fun at them, he frequently warms to their creativity: just as the sap rises at the start of the poem, so most of his characters reward the world with their contributions. Their activities might be morally questionable but their energy is never in doubt.

How strong is Chaucer's mockery? As has been suggested it may be that he can poke fun at his characters' failings without having to do so directly. Some characters fool themselves. You might consider The Prioress, The Merchant, and The Guildsmen in this way?

Sometimes Chaucer points to a physical feature which, he might well claim, has merely involved observation (*so as it semed me* [39]). But we can sense there is another purpose. This is often to reveal a character trait somehow symbolized in the feature of appearance: e.g. The Prioress's brooch (160), The Miller's nostrils (557), the emasculated bodily features of The Pardoner (688–90).

What do you think of the way that the most roguish actions are described in the most admiring language. Why did The Friar hear confession so sweetly (221), The Merchant speak with such ceremony (274), and why was The Shipman *certeinly . . . a good felawe* (395)?

One final, and fairly central point about the irony, involves tracking through the poem for references to love. The love of God should have been uppermost in the minds of these characters. Certainly there are some noble examples of love: The Knight's of chivalry; The Parson's of the souls of his parishioners, and The Clerk's of his study. But what other references are there, either direct or implied, to love? Do these references mock the idea of religious love?

Do these references suggest that the idea of religous love is being mocked? Chaicer often shows in the pilgrims a discrepancy between earthly and spiritual love. For instance, the Monk loves to hunt:

'And whan that he rood, men myghte his brydel heere
Gynglen in a whistlynge wynd als cleere
And .eek as loude as dooth the chapel belle.'   (169-71)

As a reader, you are faced with a choice of perspectives here, as elsewhere in the poem: is the Monk's love of earthly sport inappropriate, admirable or even potentially redemptive, if by example of his hunting he calls other men to God? Chaucer leaves his reader to draw their own conclusions.

Chronology

1315–16	Great Famine
1321–2	Civil War in England
1327	Deposition and death of Edward II – Accession of Edward III
1337	Start of the Hundred Years War
Early 1340s	Geoffrey Chaucer born, the son of John (a wine merchant) and Agnes – originally the family came from Ipswich
1346	Defeat of the French at Crecy
1348	Black Death
1350	Statute of Labourers' Act passed
1356–9	Page in the household of The Countess of Ulster
1359	Fought in the wars with France in the army of the Prince Lionel
1360	Captured and ransomed
1360–6	Studied law and finance at The Inns of Court; 1361 second major occurrence of plague; 1362 *Piers Plowman* published
1366	Evidence of Chaucer travelling in Europe, possibly on a pilgrimage; married (Phillipa); Chaucer's father died
1366–70	Chaucer travelled again in Europe, four times; destinations unknown but possibly including a journey to Italy; 1367 first record of Chaucer's membership of the royal household – a squire in the court
1368–72	*The Book of the Duchess* written in this period; before 1372 translated the *Roman de la Rose* (*The Romaunt of the Rose*)
1372–3	Chaucer on King's business in Italy
1374	Moved to Aldgate in London; appointed Customs Controller (to control taxes on wool, sheepskins and leather)

1376–7	Further travelling in Flanders and France on King's secret business. 1376 'Good Parliament' meets; death of Edward, the Black Prince. 1377 Death of Edward III; accession of Richard II
1378	Travelled again to Italy – renewed acquaintance with works of Italian writers
1378–80	*The House of Fame* written; 1379 Richard II introduces Poll Tax
1380–2	*The Parliament of Fowls*; 1381 Peasants' Revolt
1380s	Moved to Kent (precise date unknown)
1382–6	*Troilus and Criseyde* and *The Legend of Good Women* written. 1385 gave up post at Custom House; became Justice of the Peace
1386	Gave up house at Aldgate; election to Parliament
1387	Phillipa presumed to have died
1388–92	The *General Prologue* and earlier *Canterbury Tales* written; 1389–91 appointed to be Clerk of the King's works. 1391–2 *A Treatise on the Astrolabe* written
1392–5	Most of *The Canterbury Tales* completed
1396–1400	Later *Canterbury Tales* written; 1396 Anglo-French Treaty. 1397–9 Richard II's reign of 'tyranny'
1399	Returned to London, in a house near The Lady Chapel of Westminster Abbey; deposition of Richard II; accession of Henry IV
1400	Chaucer died (date on tomb in Westminster Abbey given as 25 October)

Further Reading

Editions

You may find that the following editions have useful notes:

L. D. Benson (ed.), *The Riverside Chaucer* (Oxford University Press, 1988).

F. N. Robinson (ed.), *The Works of Geoffrey Chaucer* (2nd ed.) (Oxford University Press, 1957).

Walter Skeat, *The Prologue to The Canterbury Tales* (Oxford University Press, 1890).

James Winny, *The General Prologue to The Canterbury Tales* (Cambridge University Press, 1965).

Biography

D. R. Howard, *Chaucer, His Life, His Works, His World* (Dutton, New York, 1987).

G. Kane, *Chaucer* (Past Masters Series) (Oxford University Press, 1984).

Criticism

Michael Alexander, *Prologue to The Canterbury Tales* (Longman, 1980).

Muriel Bowden, *A Commentary on the General Prologue to The Canterbury Tales* (New York, 1973).

This book in the series Oxford Guides to Chaucer provides a succinct and reliable account of recent scholarship:

Helen Cooper, *The Canterbury Tales* (Oxford University Press, 1989).

This book is still valuable on particular issues, though some of its conclusions have been contested:

W. C. Curry, *Chaucer and the Medieval Sciences* (London, 1960).

This book has a useful commentary:

E. T. Donaldson, (ed.) *Chaucer's Poetry* (California Press, New York, 1975).

D. R. Howard, *The Idea of The Canterbury Tales* (California Press, London, 1985)

The controversy around The Knight may be followed up in these two publications:

Terry Jones, *Chaucer's Knight* (Routledge, London, 1980).

Maurice Keen, 'Chaucer's Knight, the English Aristocracy and the Crusade' in V. J. Scattergood and J. W. Sherborne (eds.) *English Court Culture in the Later Middle Ages* (London, 1983).

This critical work revolutionized the study of the *General Prologue*:

Jill Mann, *Chaucer and Medieval Estates Satire* (Cambridge University Press, 1973).

Other useful books

D. Burnley, *A Guide to Chaucer's Language* (Methuen, London, 1983).

J. D. North, *Chaucer's Universe* (Oxford University Press, 1988).

Clair C. Olson, in Beryl Rowland (ed.) 'Chaucer and Fourteenth Century Society' in *Companion to Chaucer Studies* (Oxford University Press, Toronto, 1968).

Derek Pearsall, *The Canterbury Tales* (Unwin, 1985).

Eileen Power, *Medieval People* (Penguin, 1924).

Paul Strohm, *Social Chaucer* (Cambridge, Mass., 1989).

Historical Background

This book is very good on social background:

Maurice Keen, *English Society in the Later Middle Ages* (Penguin, 1990).

This book provides a very lively account of the period:

B. Tuchman, *A Distant Mirror: The Calamitous 14th Century* (Penguin, 1990).

Tasks

In each of the following tasks it is assumed that you will select three or four pilgrims to use as examples.

1 Is the *General Prologue* mildly ironic or heavily satirical?

2 From the portraits of the ecclesiastical pilgrims, to what extent do you find the Church corrupt?

3 With close reference to three portraits show how physical description is used as a technique in characterization.

4 Consider closely any pilgrim whose behaviour appears to contradict his or her calling in life.

5 Is it the case that Chaucer can both mock and admire his characters?

6 Are there rogues amongst the pilgrims? If so, are any of them dislikeable?

7 To what extent do you find any of the pilgrims to be vain?

8 How important is avarice as a subject of the *General Prologue*?

9 Which characters do you find genuinely good? Are any of them unrealistically good?

10 Do you admire the vitality of the characters? How is this established? Is it to be admired even when put to ill use?

11 With close reference to some of the mockery in the portraits show how Chaucer has succeeded in making the *General Prologue* humorous on occasions.

12 Having read and studied the *General Prologue*, what are some of the impressions it offers you of medieval English life?

13 Would you agree that there is sometimes a difference between the images that the pilgrims hold of themselves, and the truth revealed of their characters in the *General Prologue*?

14 Which portraits most appeal to you?

A portrait of Geoffrey Chaucer painted in the Fifteenth century, now held at
Bothwell Castle

'April from *Les Très Riches Heures du Duc de Berry*. Compare this image with the descriptions of spring in lines 1-18 and on pp. 149–50 of the Appendix

Engraving of a medieval feast from an illumination in the Luttrell Psalter: *His table dormaunt in his halle alway / Stood redy covered al the longe day* (353–4)

Squier: *Embrouded was he, as it were a meede / Al ful of fresshe floures, whyte and reede* (89–90)

Frankeleyn: *Whit was his berd as is the dayseye* (332)

Wyf of Bathe: *Upon an amblere esily she sat, / ywympled wel, and on hir heed an hat* (469)

Persoun: *A good man was ther of religioun, / And was a povre Persoun of a Toun* (477–8)

Four miniatures from the margins of the Ellesmere manuscript, illuminated within a few years of Chaucer's death

A panel from a stained glass window in Canterbury Cathedral
commemorating the many pilgrims who travelled to the shrine of St
Thomas a Becket

*The characters of Chaucer's Pilgrims are the characters which compose all
ages and nations… They are the physiognomies or lineaments of universal
human life, beyond which Nature never steps.'* wrote the writer and
engraver, William Blake, in his *Descriptive Catalogue* (1809) about the
painting from which this engraving is taken

A Note on Chaucer's English

Chaucer's English has so many similarities with Modern English that it is unnecessary to learn extensive tables of grammar. With a little practice, and using the glosses provided, it should not be too difficult to read the text. Nevertheless, it would be foolish to pretend that there are no differences. The remarks which follow offer some information, hints and principles to assist students who are reading Chaucer's writings for the first time, and to illustrate some of the differences (and some of the similarities) between Middle and Modern English. More comprehensive and systematic treatments of this topic are available in *The Riverside Chaucer* and in D. Burnley, *A Guide to Chaucer's Language*.

1 Inflections

These are changes or additions to words, usually endings, which provide information about number (whether a verb or a noun is singular or plural) tense or gender.

a) *Verbs*

In the **present** tense most verbs add –e in the first person singular (e.g. *I ryde*), –est in the second person singular (e.g. *thou sayest*), –eth in the third person singular (*she sayeth*) and –en in the plural. This can be summarized as follows:

	Middle English	Modern English
Singular	1 I telle	I tell
	2 Thou tellest	You tell
	3 He/She/It telleth	He/She/It tells
Plural	1 We tellen	We tell
	2 Ye tellen	You tell
	3 They tellen	They tell

As you can see, Middle English retains more inflections than Modern English, but the system is simple enough. Old English, the phase of the language between around 449 AD, when the Angles first came to Britain, and about 1100, had many more inflections.

In describing the **past** tense it is necessary to begin by making a distinction, which still applies in Modern English, between strong and weak verbs. **Strong verbs** form their past tense by changing their stem (e.g. I sing, I sang; You drink, you drank; he fights, he fought; we throw, we threw), while **weak verbs** add to the stem (I want, I wanted; you laugh, you laughed; he dives, he dived).

In the past tense in Middle English, strong verbs change their stems (e.g. *sing* becomes *sang* or *song*) and add –e in the second person singular (e.g. *thou songe*) and –en in the plural (e.g. *they songen*). Weak verbs add –de or –te (e.g. *fele* becomes *felte*, *here* becomes *herde)* with –st in the second person singular (e.g. *thou herdest*) and –n in the plural (e.g. *they felten*). The table below compares the past tense in Middle and Modern English for strong and weak verbs.

Strong Verbs

	Middle English Present stem: 'sing'	Modern English
Singular	1 I sange (or soonge)	I sang (or sung)
	2 Thou songe	You sang
	3 He/She/It sange	He/She/It sang
Plural	1 We songen	We sang
	2 Ye songen	You sang
	3 They songen	They sang

Weak Verbs

	Middle English Present stem: 'here'	Modern English hear
Singular	1 I herde	I heard
	2 Thou herdest	You heard
	3 He/She/It herde	He/She/It heard
Plural	1 We herden	We heard
	2 Ye herden	You heard
	3 They herden	They heard

The past tense can also be formed using the auxiliary verb *Gan* plus the past participle (e.g. *gan… preye* [301]: prayed). In a very few cases *Gan* means 'began' but in most cases it indicates a past tense. Some verbs add initial *y* to their past participle (e.g. *yronne* [8], *yfalle* [25]).

b) *Nouns and Adjectives*

Nouns mostly add –s or –es for plural (e.g. *songes* [95]) and possessive (e.g. *lordes* [47]). There are no apostrophes in Middle English! Some nouns add –en for plural (e.g. *eyen* [152]). Although (unlike modern French or German) nouns do not take grammatical gender in Middle English, some nouns do add –e for feminine (e.g. *tappestere* [241], barmaid).

Some adjectives add –e in the plural (e.g. *fresshe* [90]).

c) *Personal Pronouns*

The forms of the personal pronouns are somewhat different from those used in Modern English and are worth recording in full:

		Subject	Object	Possessive
Singular	1	I, ich	me	myn, my
	2	Thou, thow	thee	thyn, thy
	3 masculine	He	hym, him	his
	3 feminine	She	her	hir, hire
	3 neuter	It, hit	it, hit	his
Plural	1	We	us	owre, our, owres
	2	Ye	you, yow	your, youres
	3	They	hem	hire, here

Remember that the distinction between *thou* and *you* in Middle English often involves politeness and social relationship as well as number. This is similar to modern French or German. Thus *thou* forms are used with friends, family and social inferiors, *you* forms with strangers or superiors.

2 Relative Pronouns

The main **relative pronouns** found are *that* and *which*. In translating *that* it is often wise to try out a range of Modern English equivalents, such as *who, whom, which*. The prefix *ther-* in such words as *therto* and *therwith* often refers back to the subject matter of the previous phrase. *Therto* may be translated as 'in addition to all that' or 'in order to achieve that'.

3 Impersonal Construction

With certain verbs the **impersonal construction** is quite common (e.g. *Me thynketh* [37], it seems to me; *hym leste*, it pleased him[787]).

4 Reflexive Pronouns

Many verbs can be used with a **reflexive pronoun**, a pronoun which refers back to the subject (as in modern French or German) and which may, depending on the verb employed, be translated or understood as part of the verb (e.g. *born hym weel* [87], conducted himself well; *peyned hire* [139], took pains).

5 Extra Negatives

In Middle English extra **negatives** often make the negative stronger, whereas in Modern English double negatives cancel each other out (e.g. *That no drope ne fille* [131], so that no drop fell).

6 Contraction

Sometimes negatives and pronouns merge with their associated verbs (e.g. *nas* from *ne was*, was not; *artow* from *art thou*, are you).

7 Word Order

Middle English **word order** is often freer than Modern English, and in particular there is more inversion of subject and verb (e.g. *A Knyght ther was* [43], *Ful worthy was he* [47]). In analysing difficult sentences you should first locate the verb (A in the examples below), then its subject (B), then the object or complement (C). (Roughly, a verb which involves activity takes an object – he hit the ball, she gave him the book – while a verb which describes a state of affairs takes a complement – it was yellow, you look better.) Then you should put these elements together (D). It should be easier to see how the various qualifiers fit in (E).

In the sentence beginning at line 83, the verb (A) is *was*, the subject (B) *he*, the complement (C) *of evene lengthe*. Put together (D) this gives: he was moderately long. When we add the qualifier (E) *Of his stature*, this changes to: he was moderately tall. We can then see that *wonderly delyvere* (wonderfully active, or agile) and *of greet strengthe* are further complements dependent on *he was*: he was moderately tall, wonderfully active and very strong. In most cases you will not need to analyse (or construe) a sentence like this, but if you are unsure this procedure may help you. A slightly harder example, which you might like to try, would be the sentence beginning at line 35.

The main verb (A) here is the impersonal *Me thynketh*; the subject (B) is *it*: it seems to me. The complement (C) is *acordaunt to resoun*, reasonable. The resulting construction (It seems to me reasonable . . .) requires another clause to complete the complement, in this case *To telle yow al the condicioun*. Once we have the main structure (D) (It seems to me reasonable to tell you the state) we can fit in the words and phrases which qualify and develop the point: (E) But nevertheless, while I have time, before I go any further into my story, **it seems to me reasonable to tell you the state** of all of them, as it appeared to me, who they were, their status, and the clothes they wore; and I shall begin with the knight.

The sentence beginning at line 19 is a much harder example.

A and B The main verb is the first word *Bifil* (it happened). This impersonal verb implies its own subject (it).

C *Bifil* must be linked to its complement (that a company came into the inn, [23–24]).

D From there we can derive the main structure: 'When I was in Southwark, it happened that a company, who intended to go to Canterbury, came into the inn'.

E Then we can find places for the various explanatory phrases: 'One day at that time of year when **I was in Southwark** at the Tabard inn, in a very pious spirit and ready to go on my pilgrimage to Canterbury, **it happened that a company** of twenty-nine,

different sorts of people, but all pilgrims, **who** had been drawn
into association by chance and **intended to ride to Canterbury,
came into that inn** at night.'

8 Connection of Clauses

Middle English often does not indicate **connection of clauses** as
clearly as Modern English. In seeking to understand or in translating
you may need to provide connecting words. (In the last three lines of
the example above, for instance, I had to add the conjunctions *but*
and *and*, and the relative pronoun *who*). On occasion you may have
to provide verbs which have been omitted (particularly the verb 'to
be' or verbs of motion) or regularize number or tense (in some Middle
English sentences a subject can shift from singular to plural or a verb
from present to past). For example, in line 50 (*And evere honoured for
his worthynesse*) *he was* has to be understood as part of the sentence; in
lines 856–8:

> And with that word we ryden forth oure weye,
> And he bigan with right a myrie cheere
> His tale anon, and seyde as ye may heere.

Chaucer can mix the past tense with the historic present (sometimes
in telling a story we use the present tense, even though we and our
audience know that the events occurred in the past) but a Modern
English writer would have to maintain consistency at least within the
sentence and usually within the paragraph as well. Chaucer's usage
here (and with the implied words and the lack of connectives) may
well be closer to spoken English than modern formal writing could
be.

9 Change of Meaning

Although most of the words which Chaucer uses are still current
(often with different spellings) in Modern English, some of them
have changed their meaning. In lines 1–4, for example, every word
(except perhaps *engendred*: produced) corresponds to a Modern
English word (*soote* = sweet), but the usual modern meanings of
'virtue' and 'liquor' would not be appropriate here. So it is a good idea
to check the Notes or the Glossary even for words which look

familiar. If you are interested in investigating the ways in which words change their meanings over time you can look at the quotations provided in large historical dictionaries, such as the *Oxford English Dictionary* or the *Shorter Oxford Dictionary* or in R. W. Burchfield, *The English Language* (Oxford, 1985), pp. 113–23, or G. Hughes, *Words in Time: A Social History of English Vocabulary* (Oxford, Blackwell). Here are a few more examples from the *General Prologue*:

Middle English	(line no.)	Meaning	Equivalent modern word
array	(41)	clothing, dress	array
aventure	(844)	chance	adventure
baillif	(603)	farm manager	bailiff
barge	(410)	ship, sea-going merchant vessel	barge
burdoun	(673)	bass accompaniment	burden
bynne	(593)	grain bin	bin[1]
carpe	(474)	talk	carp[2]
catel	(373)	property	cattle
clennesse	(506)	purity	cleanness
clerk	(285)	educated person, scholar	clerk
complexioun	(333)	temperament	complexion
cordial	(443)	medicine for the heart	cordial
countrefete	(139)	imitate	counterfeit
coy	(119)	quiet	coy
croppes	(7)	shoots (of plants)	crops
curious	(196, 577)	skilful, skilfully made	curious

1 In Modern English 'bin' on its own means 'rubbish bin'.

2 'Carp' is quite a rare word in Modern English, but it means 'complain', as in 'stop carping', where the Middle English word denotes speaking generally.

A Note on Pronunciation

The *General Prologue*, like other poems, benefits from being read aloud. Even if you read it aloud in a Modern English pronunciation you will get more from it, but Middle English was pronounced differently (the sounds of a language change over time at least as much as the vocabulary or the constructions) and it helps to make some attempt at a Middle English accent. The best way to learn this is to imitate one of the recordings (the tapes issued by Pavilion and Argo are especially recommended for this purpose). A few principles are given below, more can be found in *The Riverside Chaucer*.

1 In most cases you should pronounce all consonants (for example you should sound the 'k' in knight and the 'l' in half). But in words of French origin initial 'h' (as in *hostelrye*, [23], for example) should not be sounded, nor should 'g' in the combination 'gn' (as in *digne*, [141]). The combination 'gh', (as in *draughte* [135]), is best sounded 'ch' as in Modern English 'loch'.

2 In most cases all vowels are sounded, though a final 'e' may be silent because of elision with a vowel following (e.g. do not sound the second 'e' in *veyne in*, [3]) or because of the stress pattern of the line (e.g. in line 13, I would make the second 'e' in *palmeres* silent, but sound the final 'e' in *straunge*).

3 Two points of spelling affect pronunciation. When 'y' appears as a vowel, you should sound it as 'i' (see table on page 139). Sometimes a 'u' sound before 'n' or 'm' was written 'o' (because 'u' and 'n' looked very similar in the handwriting of the time). This means that *song* and *yong* should be pronounced 'sung' and 'yung'. This also applies in *comen* and *sonne* (as in their Modern English equivalents 'come' and 'son').

4 You will not go too far wrong with combinations of vowels, such as *ai*, *eu*, and *oy* if you sound them as in Modern English. There are significant exceptions (for example *hous* [252] and *mous* [144] should be pronounced with an *oo* sound) but it is not possible to establish reliable rules purely on the basis of the spelling.

138

5 The principal vowel sounds differ somewhat from Modern English. They are set out in the table below (adapted from Norman Davis's table in *The Riverside Shakespeare*). The table distinguishes long and short versions of each vowel. This distinction still applies in Modern English (consider the 'a' sounds in hat and father) but unfortunately it is often only possible to decide whether a particular vowel is long or short by knowing about the derivation of the word. Do not despair. Even a rough approximation will help you. Only experts in Middle English and related medieval languages have reliable Middle English accents, and even they cannot be sure that Chaucer would approve them.

Vowel	Middle English example	Modern equivalent sound
Long 'a'	stables(28) caas(323)	'a' in father
Short 'a'	Ram(8) nature(11)	'a' in hat
Long 'e'	he(45) been(64)	'a' in fate
Open 'e'	teche(308) heeth(606)	'e' in there
Short 'e'	tendre(7) wende(16)	'e' in set
Unstressed 'e'	sonne(7) londes(14)	'a' in about, 'e' in forgotten
Long 'i'	I(20) ryde(27)	'i' in machine
Short 'i'	licour(3) knyght(42)	'i' in sit
Long 'o'	fro(44) goode(74)	'o' in note
Open 'o'	hooly(17) goon(12)	'oa' in broad
Short 'o'	wol(42) croppes(7)	'o' in hot
Long 'u'	flour(4) foweles(9)	'oo' in boot
Short 'u'	ful(22) juste(96)	'u' in put

Glossary

This glossary is not absolutely comprehensive. It does not record all inflected forms (see A Note on Chaucer's English p. 131) nor all variant spellings. If you do not find a word here, try sounding it out, or try minor modifications of spelling (such as 'i' for 'y', 'a' for 'o', 'ea' for 'ee', and vice versa). A few of the glosses in the commentary are not repeated in the glossary. Generally the main meaning *in this text* comes first, while more specialized meanings are given line references. Proper names which are explained in the notes do not appear in the glossary. In compiling this glossary I have relied on L. D. Benson (ed.), *The Riverside Chaucer* and on N. Davis (ed.), *A Chaucer Glossary*, which offer fuller explanations than I can here. I have also consulted the *Oxford English Dictionary* and *The Middle English Dictionary*.

aboute around
absolucioun absolution, forgiveness of sins
achaat buying
achatours buyers
accorde agreement, decision
acord agree
acordaunt agreeing
adrad afraid
aferd afraid
affile smooth
after according to (125), towards (136)
agayn against
al although
al all, entirely
ale-stake pub-sign
als as
alderbest best of all
algate always
alwey always, continually
alyght dismounted, arrived
amblere ambling horse
amorwe in the morning
anlaas dagger
anon immediately
apes fools, dupes
apiked trimmed
apothecaries pharmacists

areste stop
arette attribute to, impute
aright certainly, exactly
array clothing, dress
arrerage arrears
arwe arrow
ascendent planet coming over the horizon
asonder apart
assoillyng absolution
astored provided
atones at one time
atte at
aught all
avaunce profit
avaunt assertion, boast
aventure chance
avys consideration
awe reverence, fear
ay always, continually

bacheler apprentice knight (80)
baar, bar carried, wore
bad asked, told
baillif farm manager
bargaynes deals (sales and purchases)
barge ship, sea-going merchant vessel

barres stripes
bataille battle
bawdryk baldric, shoulder-strap
bedes beads
beggestere beggar-woman
ben are
benefice church job
benygne kind, considerate
berd beard
bet better
bifalle happen, (*bifil* 19)
biforn before, in front of, ahead (572)
bigonne began, sat at the head of (53)
bisette used
bisides near, in addition
bisily earnestly
bismotered bespattered
bit bids, commands
bitwixe between
blake black
blankmanger mousse (see Notes p. 55, line 387)
blisful happy, blessed (17)
blithe happy, pleased
bokeler small shield
boote remedy
boras borax
bord table
born hym conducted himself
bracer arm guard
brawn muscle
breem freshwater bream
breeth breath
bretful brimful
bretherhed guild, confraternity
brode plainly
brood broad, wide
broun brown, dark
brustles bristles
brymstoon sulphur
burdoun bass accompaniment
burgeys burgess, member of the city council
but only, except
but if unless
bynne grain bin
byte burn, scour
byynge buying

caas cases, eventuality, chance
carf carved
carl rogue
carpe talk
catel property
ceint belt
celle subordinate house
ceruce white lead
chambre bedroom
chaped mounted
chapeleyne secretary
chapman merchant
charge burden, responsibility
charitee Christian love, goodwill
chaunce event, fortune
chaunterie chantry, job singing masses
cheere manners, behaviour, expression
cherubynnes cherub's
chevyssaunce financial arrangements, borrowings
chiere welcome, greeting
chyvachie cavalry expedition
clad covered, clothed, bound (294)
cleere clearly
clene cleanly, brightly (367)
clennesse purity
clepe call, name, say (643)
clerk educated person, scholar
cloysterer monk
cloystre cloister
cofre coffer, money-chest
colerik choleric (see Notes p. 51, line 333)
colpons strands
compeer companion
complexioun temperament (see Notes p. 51, line 333)
composicioun agreement
condicioun state, circumstances
conseil secrets, decision (784)
contour auditor
contree district
cop tip
cope long cloak, cape
coppe cup
corage courage, heart, spirit, inclination
cordial medicine for the heart

141

cosyn closely related
cote tunic, coat
countrefete imitate
cours course
courtepy jacket
covenaunt agreement, contract
coverchiefs headcoverings
covyne deceit
coy quiet
craft skill, profession
cristen Christian
cristendom Christendom, Christian countries
croppes shoots (of plants)
croys cross
crulle curled
cryke creek, inlet
curat parish priest
cure care
curious skilful, skilfully made
curteis courteous
curteisie courtesy, good manners
cut lot

daliaunce sociable talk, flirting
daunce dance
daunger control (663)
daungerous haughty, aloof
dayerye dairy cattle
decree decretal, law of the church
deed dead
degree rank, social class
delit delight, pleasure
delyvere agile
delve dig
desdeyn indignation
despitous scornful
desport amusement
dettelees without debts
devout pious
devys scheme, wishes
devyse tell
deyntee fine, superior
deyntees delicacies
deys dais
digne worthy, haughty (517)
dischevelee with hair unbound
discreet judicious
disport entertainment
dokked cut short

dong dung
doomes judgements
dormant permanently in place
dorste dared
double worstede thick, expensive cloth
dresse arrange, care for, prepare
draughte draught, the quantity of liquid taken at one swallow
drogges drugs
droghte drought
drouped fell short
dyke make ditches
dyvyne divine, holy

ecclesiaste churchman
ech each
eek also
embrouded embroidered
encombred stuck
endite write poetry (95), draft documents (325)
engendred produced
enoynt anointed, rubbed with oil
ensample example
entuned intoned
envyned stocked with wine
er before
ercedekenes archdeacon's
erly early
erst first
erys ears
eschaunge exchange, market
ese comfort, pleasure
estaat condition, position in society
estatly, estatlich dignified
esy lenient
esy of dispence moderate in spending
evene moderate
everichon everyone, all
everemoore always
everydeel every part, altogether
excellence exceptional talent

facultee professional dignity
faire well, beautifully, handsomely, neatly
faldyng coarse woollen cloth
famulier familiar
farsed stuffed

fayn gladly
fee symple absolute possession
felawe companion
felaweshipe fellowship
felicitee happiness
fer far, at a distance
ferme fee, rent
ferne distant
ferre farther
ferther further
ferthyng farthing (quarter-penny), drop (134)
festne fasten
fetisly elegantly
feyne invent
fille fell
fithele fiddle
Flaundres Flanders
flessh meat
flex flax
flour flower
flour-de-lys lily
floytynge playing the flute
foo foe, enemy, opponent
foot-mantel overskirt
forneys furnace, oven, fire (202)
forpyned tormented
forster forester
fortunen calculate
forward agreement
fother cartload
foweles birds
frankeleyn free man, landowner
fraternitee confraternity, guild
fredom generosity, nobleness
fressh new, young, blooming, vigorous
fro from
ful very
fustian coarse cloth

galyngale a root used in flavouring
game sport
gat-tothed with teeth set wide apart
gauded with large beads
gay finely dressed, splendid, bright
geere equipment, cutlery (352)
gentil noble
gerland garland
gerner granary

gesse suppose, perceive
gipser purse
girdle belt
girt encircled
gise manner
glarynge staring
gobet piece
goliardeys buffoon, joker
good wealth, property (611)
goon go
goost spirit
governaunce behaviour, rule, control
graunt agree
graunt grant, privilege
grece grease
gretter larger
grope test, question
ground texture
grounded instructed
grys squirrel-fur
gyde guide
gynglen jingle
gypon tunic

haberdasshere haberdasher, seller of clothing accessories
habergeon coat of mail
halwe saint, shrine (14)
hardily certainly
hardy brave, tough
harlot rascal
harlotries indecency
harm misfortune, pain, pity (385)
harneised mounted, ornamented
harre hinge
haunt practice, skill (447), usual place (252b)
havenes harbours (407)
heed head
heede notice (303)
heeld held, considered, followed (176)
heep lot, crowd
heeth heath, open land
hem them
hente obtain
herberwe shelter, lodging, harbour (403), inn (765)
herkneth listen

hertely cordially
herys hairs
hethenesse heathen countries
hewe colour
hierde herdsman
highte called
hir their
hir, hire her
hire money, payment
holden considered
holp help
holt wood
holwe hollow, emaciated
hond hand, wrist
honest honourable, respectable
hoole whole
hoomly simply
hoote hotly, passionately
hosen stockings
hostelrye inn
hostiler innkeeper
humour type of bodily fluid
hy serious
hyndreste last
hyne servant

ilke same
infect invalidated
inspire breathe life into (6)
iren iron

janglere chatterer, teller of tales
japes tricks
jet fashion
jolitee ease
juste joust
justice judge

kan knows
keep, kep notice (in the phrase 'take keep')
kepe take care of, preserve, ensure (130), protect (276)
kepere supervisor
knarre rugged fellow
knyght of the shire member of parliament representing the county
knobbes lumps
koude knew (how to)

kouthe could
kowthe known

laas cord
large freely (734)
lat let
latoun latten, brass
lazar leper
leed cauldron
leet allowed, let
lene lean
lengthe height (83)
lest desire, pleasure
letuaries electuaries, medicines
levere rather
lewed ignorant
licenciat licensed
licour liquid
lipsed lisped
liste wanted, preferred (often used impersonally)
lite little, small
lodemenage pilotage
lond land
loore teaching
lordynges sirs, gentlemen
love-dayes days on which disputes were resolved
lowely humble, modest
luce pike
lust pleasure, delight
lusty lively
lymytour limiter (see Notes p. 44, line 209)
lystes lists, venue for tournaments
lytarge lead monoxide
lyveree uniform (of the guild 363)

maistrie mastery, control
maladye illness
male bag
maunciple business agent
maner sort
manhod manliness
mantel cloak
marchal master of ceremonies
martir martyr
marybones marrow bones
medlee parti-coloured
meede meadow

meeke meek, humble
mercenarie hireling
mere mare
meschief trouble
mesurable moderate
mete food, mealtime
mo more
mormal ulcer, running sore
mortreux thick soup or stew
morwe morning
mottelee cloth of mixed colour
moyste supple
muchel much
murierly more pleasantly
murye merry, pleasing
muwe pen for birds
myght power
myre mire, bog
myrthe mirth, amusement,
  happiness
myscarie come to grief
myster trade

namoore no more
narwe narrow
nas was not
nat not
nathelees nevertheless
ne not, and . . . not, nor
neet cattle
noght not, not at all, nothing
nones occasion
noot do not know
norissyng nourishment
nosethirles nostrils
not heed close-cropped head
note voice
nowthe now
ny near, close
nyce scrupulous
nyghtertale night-time

o one
office secular job
offrynge offering, collection (450),
  priest's income from collection
  (489)
oille of tartre cream of tartar
oon one
oon, after uniformly good
ooth oath

ounces small strands
outrely absolutely
outridere outrider, monk with
  business outside the monastery
over al everywhere
overeste uppermost
over-lippe upper lip
overspradde covered
owher anywhere
oynement ointment

paas walking speed (825)
pace go, surpass (574)
palfrey horse
pardee by God, to be sure
parfit perfect
parisshens parishioners
partrich partridge
pass go, pass by, surpass
patente letter of appointment
penaunce penance (see Notes to
  The Pardoner p. 69)
peire set
perced pierced
pers grey-blue
persoun parson
pestilence plague
peyned hire took pains
phisik medicine
piled hairless
pilwe-beer pillowcase
pitaunce gift, payment
pitous compassionate
plentevous abundant
pleyen to play
pleyn full, entirely
pomely dappled
poraille poor people
port manner, behaviour
post pillar
pouch purse
poudre-marchant tart a sharp-
  flavoured spice
poure pore over
povre poor
poynaunt sharp, spicy
poynt condition
praktisour practitioner
prelaat prelate, high-ranking
  churchman

presse cupboard, curler (81), casting mould (263)
prikasour hunter
priketh spurs, stimulates
prikyng tracking
pris, prys value, reputation, price (815), prize (237)
propre own
proprely appropriately, correctly
pryvely secretly
pulled plucked
purchace buy property
purchas income
purchasour land-buyer
purfiled lined with fur
purtreye draw, describe
pynche at find an error in
pynched pleated

quyk vivid (306)
quyk-silver mercury

rage sport, frolic
raughte reached
recchelees careless
recorde remind, recall
rede read, interpret (741)
reed red
reed advisor (665)
reeve estate manager
reherce repeat
rekene reckon, calculate
rekenynge account
remenaunt remainder
rennyng running
rente rent, income
reportour record keeper
resoun reason
reverence respect, dignity, ceremony (525)
reysed ridden on raids
riche richly (609)
roialliche royally, splendidly
rood rode
roost roast
roote root, cause
rote stringed instrument
rote, by by heart
rouncy horse, carthorse
route company
rudeliche crudely

sangwyn sanguine (see Notes p. 51, line 333), red (439)
saucefleem pimpled
saugh saw
sautrie psaltery (a stringed instrument, like a small harp)
save apart from
scalled scabby
scarsly economically
scathe pity
science knowledge
sclendre thin
scoleye attend university
see sea
seege siege
seeke sick (18)
seigh saw
seke, seche seek
semely beautiful, comely, elegant(ly)
semycope short cloak
semyly properly (151)
sendal thin silk
sentence meaning, significance
servysable attentive, willing to serve
sessiouns law courts, court hearings
sethe simmer
shamefastnesse modesty
shapen yow intend
shaply suitable, fit
sheeld écu, unit of exchange (see Notes p. 47, line 278)
sheene bright
shire county
shirreve sheriff
shiten filthy
sho shoe
shoures showers
shyne shin
sike sick
sikerly certainly, surely
sire master
sithes times
slee kill
sleighte tricks
smerte suffer (230), painfully (149)
smoot beat
smothe smoothly
sobrely gravely, seriously

solaas delight
solempne dignified
solempnely ceremoniously,
  pompously
somdel somewhat
somtyme once
sondry various
sonne sun
soore severely, bitterly
soote sweet, fragrant
soothly truly
sop piece of bread
soper supper
sort luck
soun sound
souple supple
Southwerk Southwark
sownynge sounding, agreeing with
  (see Notes p. 47, line 275)
space time, opportunity, course
  (176)
spak spoke
spanne span, about 18–23 cm.
spare refrain, hold back
sparwe sparrow
speede prosper
spiced delicate, over-particular
spores spurs
sprynge break, begin
stature height
stemed gleamed
stepe prominent, bright
stif strong
stoor livestock
stot horse
stout strong
straunge foreign
streit strict, narrow
streite tightly
strem river, current (402)
strike hank
stronde shore
studieth deliberate, brood, study
stuwe fishpond
stywardes stewards
substaunce wealth, pay (489)
subtilly cunningly
suffisaunce sufficiency
suffre allow

superfluitee excess
surcote outer coat
swerd sword
swetely gently, in a kindly manner
swich such
swyn pigs
swynk work
symple unaffected, innocent
syn since

tabard loose upper garment
Tabard the Tabard inn
taffata taffeta, a type of silk
taille, by on credit
takel equipment
talen tell stories
tappestere barmaid
tapycer weaver of tapestries and
  rugs
targe shield
taryynge delay
temple Inn of Court, lawyers'
  college
tendre tender, young
termes law reports (323),
  expressions (639)
thanne then
ther there, where
theron on it
therto to it, about it, in addition,
  also
thilke that same
tho those
thries three times
thriftily properly, carefully
til to
tithe tenth, proportion due to the
  Church
toft tuft
tollen charge, take payment
tretys well-formed
trompe trumpet
trouthe fidelity, loyalty, honour
trowe believe
trussed packed
tukked hitched up
tweye two
twynne part, go
typet point of the hood

undergrowe small, underdeveloped
undertake declare
untrewe falsely, inaccurately
usage customs

vavasour sub-vassal (sse Notes p. 53, line 360)
venerie hunting
vernycle badge from the pilgrimage to Rome
verray true
vertu power (4)
vertuous virtuous, capable
veyne vein
viage voyage, journey
vigilies, vigils services and feasts held the night before holy days
vileynye boorishness, vulgarity, rude words (70)
visage face
vitaille victuals, provisions
voirdit verdict
vouche sauf agree

wait (wayte) expect, take care (571)
walet travel bag
wantowne jolly, pleasure-loving
wantownesse affectation
war aware, prudent (309)
wastel-breed fine white bread
webbe weaver
weel well
wende go
werk do
werre war
werte wart
wex wax
weye road, journey
weyeden weighed
whan when
whelkes pimples
whelp puppy
wherwith the wherewithal, (money) with which
whilom once, formerly
wight man
wiste knew, expected

wit intelligence
withholde retained, employed
withouten not counting
wodecraft woodcraft, forestry, gamekeeping
wol will
wolde wanted, would
wonderly marvellously
wone custom
wonyng living, dwelling
wood mad
woot know
worthy deserving, respectable, distinguished
wrighte workman
wroghte made, did
wrooth angry
wyde wide, spacious (28), large (491)
wympul wimple, garment covering the whole head but leaving the face visible
wynne earn money
wynnyng earnings, profit
wys wise, prudent

yaf gave
ydrawe drawn, taken
ye eye
yeddynges ballads
yeldehalle guildhall
yeldynge yield
yemanly skilfully, in a yeomanly fashion
yerde stick
yeve give
yfalle fallen
ygo gone
yive give
ylad hauled
ymage talisman (418)
ynogh enough
yonge young
yronne run
yshadwed shaded
yteyd laced, tied
ywympled covered with a wimple
ywroght made

Appendix

History of the Destruction of Troy

Guido delle Colonne completed his Latin prose *History of the Destruction of Troy* in 1287. Chaucer certainly knew it and used some details from it in his long poem on the Troy legend, *Troilus and Criseyde* (completed about 1385). Compare this translated passage from the beginning of Guido's fourth book with the first sentence of the *General Prologue*.

> It was the time when the sun . . . had already begun its journey through the sign of Aries, when the spring equinox is celebrated, when the weather begins to entice eager mortals into the clear fresh air. At that time the ice has broken and the mildly blowing West wind ripples the waters, the springs begin to flow, the moisture exhaled from the earth is drawn up to treetops and the tips of branches. From these the seeds sprout, the seedlings grow, the meadows become green, adorned with the different coloured flowers. The trees all around send forth new leaves, the earth is covered in grass, the birds sing and make music in the modulation of sweet harmony. Then almost half the month of April has passed...
>
> (translated from Guido delle Colonne's *Historia destructionis Troiae* ed. M. E. Griffin [1936])

Roman de la Rose

The *Roman de la Rose*, an Old French poem and one of the most influential works of the later Middle Ages sets out in allegorical form the whole art of love. The poem was begun around 1237 by the courtly poet Guillaume de Lorris. About forty years after Guillaume's death the scholar Jean de Meun vastly enlarged and completed the work in a somewhat earthier style. Chaucer himself made a translation of the *Roman de la Rose* (called *The Romaunt of the Rose*) and its influence has been traced in many of his works.

The first translated extract is a description of a May morning from the beginning of the poem. Compare this with the opening sentence of the *General Prologue*.

149

I realised that it was May, a good five years ago, or even more.
I dreamed that we were in May, the joyful time of love, the time
when everyone is happy, when every bush and hedge is covered
with new leaves. The woods, which are so dry while winter lasts,
recover their green. The earth itself becomes proud because of the
dew which waters it, and forgets the poverty it has been in all winter.
When the earth becomes so vain that it wants to have a new dress
with a hundred pairs of colours in the grass, and the flowers of blue,
white and other colours . . . The birds which were silent and cold in
the bitter weather of winter are so joyful because of the fair weather
of May. They feel compelled to sing in order to show how much joy
they have in their hearts. The nightingales must sing loudly; the
parrot and lark revive and satiate themselves in joy. The joyous
beautiful weather makes young men feel themselves happy and
amorous. The person who does not feel love in May, when he hears
the sweet piteous songs of the birds on their branches, has a very
hard heart.   (45–83)

The second translated extract is from Jean de Meun's continuation.
La Vieille, an older and somewhat cynical woman, is explaining the
part played in the art of seduction by table manners. Compare Chaucer's description of The Prioress at table (127–136).

Let her take care never to dip her fingers deeply (as far as the joint)
into the sauce, never to cover her lips in soup, garlic or fat, never to
take too large a morsel, or stuff too much in her mouth. When she
has to dip a piece of meat in the sauce, of whatever kind, she
should hold it with her fingertips and carry it carefully to her mouth,
so that no drop of soup, sauce or pepper falls on her breast. Let her
drink so carefully that she spills nothing on herself. Anyone seeing
her spill her drink might think her ill-educated or greedy. She must
not touch her glass while she has food in her mouth. She should
wipe her lips clean, especially the upper lip, because if any grease
remains there, drops of it will appear in her wine, which is ugly and
dirty.   (13408–32)

(translated from Guillaume de Lorris and Jean de Meun's
Le Roman de la Rose ed. D. Poiriou [Paris, 1974])

Piers Plowman

Piers Plowman is a Middle English allegorical poem composed in four versions (known as Z, A, B and C) by William Langland between about 1362 and 1390. The prologue to *Piers Plowman* contains a description of fourteenth century English society which may be placed beside Chaucer's *General Prologue*. The continuous extract from Walter Skeat's edition of the B text, printed below, includes Langland's discussions of the friars, a pardoner and corrupt parish priests. Similar material appears in Chaucer's accounts, and it is possible that an early version of *Piers Plowman* was among Chaucer's sources. Compare the attitude of the observer in *Piers Plowman* to that of the pilgrim Chaucer (208–69, 496–514, 669–714). In what way are Langland's criticisms of parish priests reflected in Chaucer's praise of his Parson?

> I fonde there freris alle the foure ordres,
> Preched the peple for profit of hem-selven,
> Glosed the gospel as hem good lyked,   60
> For coveitise of copis construed it as thei wolde.
> Many of this maistres freris mowe clothen hem at lykyng,
> For here money and marchandise marchen togideres.
> For sith charite hath be chapman and chief to shryve lordes,
> Many ferlis han fallen in a fewe yeris.   65
> Bot holychirche and hii holde better togideres,
> The moste myschief on molde is mountyng wel faste.

60 **Glosed** commented on, explained   63 **marchandise** business
64 **chapman** businessman   64 **shryve** give confession to
65 **ferlis** wonders   67 **myschief** harm   67 **molde** earth

> There preched a pardonere as he a prest were,
> Broughte forth a bulle with bishopes seles,
> And seide that hym-self myghte assoilen hem alle   70
> Of falshed of fastyng of vowes ybroken.
> Lewed men leved hym wel and lyked his wordes,
> Comen up knelyng to kissen his bulles;
> He bonched hem with his brevet and blered here eyes,
> And raughte with his ragman rynges and broches.   75

Thus they geven here golde glotones to kepe,
And leveth such loseles that lecherye haunten.
Were the bischop yblissed and worth bothe his eres,
His seel shulde nought be sent to deceyve the peple.
Ac it is naught by the bischop that the boy precheth,   80
For the parisch prest and the pardonere parten the silver,
That the poraille of the parisch sholde have if thei nere.

69 **bulle** document   70 **assoilen** absolve   72 **Lewed** ignorant
72 **leved** believed   74 **bonched** struck   74 **brevet** letter of indulgence
74 **blered** dimmed   75 **raughte** obtained   75 **ragman** document
77 **loseles** rascals   77 **haunten** indulge in   80 **boy** rogue

Persones and parisch prestes pleyned hem to the bischop,
That here parisshes were pore sith the pestilence tyme,
To have a lycence and a leve at London to dwelle,   85
And syngen there for symonye for silver is swete.
Bischopes and bachelers bothe maistres and doctours,
That han cure under Criste and crounyng in tokne
And signe that thei sholden shryven here paroschienes,
Prechen and prey for hem and the pore fede,   90
Liggen in London in lenten an elles.
Somme serven the kyng and his silver tellen,
In cheker and in chancerye chalengen his dettes
Of wardes and wardmotes, weyves and streyves.
And some serven as servantz lordes and ladyes,   95
And in stede of stuwardes sytten and demen.
Here masse and here matynes and many of here oures
Arn don undevoutlych; drede is at the laste
Lest Crist in consistorie acorse ful manye.   (58–99)

(extracts from the B text in *Piers Plowman in Three
Parallel Texts* ed. Walter Skeat [OUP, 1886])

83 **pleyned** complained   84 **pestilence** plague   85 **leve** permission
86 **symonye** selling the offices of the church   87 **bachelers** graduates
88 **cure** responsibility for souls   88 **crounyng** tonsure   92 **tellen** count
93 **cheker** the court of Exchequer   93 **chalengen** demand payment of
94 **wardes** royal wards   94 **wardmotes** local meetings
94 **weyves** lost property   94 **streyves** stray animals   96 **stede** place
96 **demen** judge   98 **don** performed   99 **consistorie** church court (but
Christ's court is the last judgement)